"Look, there she is. I was right about the new neighbors having a girl," Linda Jean said excitedly. She pointed to the car that had just pulled into the driveway down the street. "It's a girl. And she looks about our age."

We all huddled around my bedroom window to see what the new girl looked like. She was peeking out of the car's sunroof. Her beautiful red hair seemed to flow forever.

"It looks like we just may have a new member of The Forever Friends Club," Joy said with a mischievous grin. "I can't wait to meet her."

"Me, too!" I said. I was eager to find out what kind of talent she would bring to Party Time. Maybe she was a great gymnast or a skateboarder or a trick bike rider.

Then a question suddenly occurred to me. She would want to be our friend, wouldn't she?

**Look for more fun times
with The Forever Friends Club:**

# New Friend Blues

Cindy Savage

Cover illustration by Richard Kriegler

*For Leann—*
*thank you for being a very special part of my life*

Published by Willowisp Press, Inc.
401 E. Wilson Bridge Road, Worthington, Ohio 43085

Copyright ©1990 by Willowisp Press, Inc.

All rights reserved. No portion of this book may be reproduced, stored in a retrieval system, or transmitted, in any form or by any means, electronic, mechanical, photocopying, recording, or otherwise without prior written permission from the publisher.

Printed in the United States of America
10 9 8 7 6 5 4 3 2 1

ISBN 0-87406-439-2

# One

"HEY, guys, the new neighbors are moving in," I said, leaning as far as I could out of my bedroom window. I was dying to get a peek at the new family. "Wouldn't it be great if they had a kid our age?"

"Yeah. It would be fun to have someone new to talk to," Joy said. "And if it was a girl, maybe she would want to join our club."

"Before we get too excited about a new girl, don't you think we should find out if the new family even has kids?" Aimee asked reasonably.

"Spoil sport," Joy said. "It's fun just to dream up what the new family will be like. Just think, maybe they'll have gorgeous boy twins or the parents will be famous circus performers or race car drivers..."

"Joy, you are a riot," I said with a giggle. "I would settle for those gorgeous boy twins you mentioned."

"Yeah, you could take one, and I could take the other," Linda Jean offered.

"And what about me?" Aimee added, pretending to pout. "I don't want to be left out of this adventure."

"Aimee, you have Graham. And you know how special he can be," I reminded her.

Aimee smiled. She and Graham really weren't officially boyfriend and girlfriend, but they had a lot of fun together. They were more like special friends.

It was early morning, and we had just awakened after a long night of giggles and fun. It had been a long time since the Forever Friends had had a sleep-over party.

"It doesn't seem like very long ago that Linda Jean's family pulled up in a moving van," Joy recalled. "I can't believe you've lived here over two years already."

"Me, neither," I said. "Hey, look. The movers are unloading a flashy, 10-speed bicycle."

Linda Jean came up beside me to see what was going on. "I wonder when the family is going to show up," she said.

Aimee was peering over my shoulder. "Don't get your hopes up too soon. Adults like to ride bikes, too."

"Come on, think positive!" Linda Jean urged. "It would be fun to have someone on the block who is newer than I am to the neighborhood. Just keep thinking *kid, kid, kid.*" She giggled and picked up one of the pillows from my bed. She swung and meant to hit Aimee, but instead managed to sideswipe my head.

"Stop. No pillow fights," I protested. "After all, we are supposed to be responsible business women. We should be spending our time doing something important. Instead, we're clowning around and spending the last few hours of our sleep-over party having a pillow fight."

They all stopped in mid-swing and stared at me like I might be really serious. But after a few seconds, they grabbed their pillows and began swinging again—and mostly at me!

Linda Jean was the first to bail out of the battle. She lowered her pillow and looked at Aimee. "I think Krissy has a point about being silly," she said seriously. "She is pretty smart, you know. I mean, she even skipped a grade in school."

"I guess you're right," Aimee agreed. "We should be able to think of something else to do." She tossed her pillow on my bed.

"Tickle fight!" they both yelled at the same time as they charged at me.

I leapt over my bed and heaved a sleeping bag in their path. But Joy was coming at me from the opposite direction. I was doomed.

In the middle of shrieks and squeals, I heard a horn honking outside.

"Wait. Stop!" I yelled, panting. "Maybe that's the new neighbors."

"You'd better be right," Linda Jean said, leaping back over the bed and heading for the window. Joy and Aimee were close behind her. I stayed behind them in case they decided to turn around and tickle me again.

I could see that a blue sports car was parked in the driveway next to the moving van. A man standing beside it looked like he was wearing an Air Force uniform. I thought he might be based at Dobbins Air Force Base outside Atlanta. Beside the man was a woman wearing a business suit—the kind my mom wears when she has an important appointment. It looked like they had been to some kind of fancy occasion.

"Look, there she is. I was right," Linda Jean said. She pointed to the open sunroof on the car. "It's a girl. And she looks about our age."

We all stared at the girl who was peeking out of the car's sunroof. She had beautiful red hair that seemed to flow forever.

"It looks like we just may have a new member of the Forever Friends Club," Joy said with a mischievous grin. "I can't wait to meet her."

"Me, too," said Aimee.

Being a member of the Forever Friends Club is the absolute best! Joy Marshall, Aimee Lawrence, and I, Krissy Branch, have lived on Honeybee Court in Atlanta since we were babies. And we've all been great friends for as long as we can remember. Linda Jean Jacobs joined our club two years ago when she and her dad moved here from California.

As club members, we meet at Joy's house every day after school and during summer vacations. We do things that normal 12-year-old girls do, like talk about boys and all the hottest TV shows. But we also work. We have our own business called Party Time. We plan parties for little kids' birthdays and celebrations, including the entertainment. And in between parties, we help out Joy's mom, Abby, who runs her own catering business.

"I wonder what kind of fun talent the new girl could bring to Party Time," Aimee said.

"Well, Party Time already has a clown," Joy said with a giggle, looking at me. "And Aimee's our craft expert. Linda Jean is great at science projects and animal shows. And I plan to keep my spot as number one dancer."

"That's fine with us, Joy," Aimee added.

"From the looks of things, she is a terrific thrower," I said. We all glanced down to the driveway. The girl had gotten out of the car and was tossing books, clothes, shoes, and papers through the air. She was yelling something that I was glad we couldn't hear. And her parents were yelling back at her. I was kind of embarrassed to be watching such a private scene, and I thought it was weird that they would scream at each other in the driveway.

"Wow, I can't believe that," I said finally.

"I'm glad that doesn't happen at my house," Joy said. "I'd be a nervous wreck from all that arguing."

After a few minutes, the red-haired girl stomped off toward the street and sat down on the curb. She put her head down on her knees.

"It looks like she's crying," Linda Jean said. "Should we go down and talk to her?"

"Maybe we should leave her alone for a while," I suggested. "It might be embarrassing for her to meet us when she's crying. I know I wouldn't want my nose to be running if I met a bunch of girls."

"Yeah, I guess you're right," Linda Jean said. "I just want to help her. I don't want her first day in a new place to be horrible. I know how it feels to be scared about moving."

"Well, let's clean up this place and get dressed. Then we'll go meet her," I said. "She'll probably be feeling a little better by then."

"Hey, maybe we could take her one of Abby's special fruit and bran muffins to welcome her to the block," Joy suggested. Joy and her mom were more like friends than mother and daughter. So, Joy and everyone else called her mom by her first name, Abby.

We all knew each others' bedrooms as well as we did our own, so cleaning up the mess we had made was a snap.

I looked over at Linda Jean, who seemed to be a million miles away. "Linda Jean, what are you thinking about?" I asked. "Are you worried about the new girl?"

"I keep thinking about what it was like to leave all my old friends and my school. And it was so hard to leave my mom and move far away from her," Linda Jean remembered. Then she smiled. "But that's all changed now, because my mom lives here and you are the best friends in the world."

"Flattery is not going to get you out of helping me straighten up this bed," Aimee said, attempting to cheer up Linda Jean. "Here, grab a pillow."

About half an hour later, we walked downstairs for a breakfast of muffins, cereal, and scrambled eggs that my mom had fixed for us. We had a party scheduled that afternoon for six-year-old Jonathan Lambert, so we needed plenty of energy. We were excited about the party, because we had come up with a neat relay racing theme.

I finished eating and took my dishes to the sink. I glanced out the kitchen window to see if the girl was still sitting on the curb.

"Is she still there?" Joy asked.

"Yep," I answered. "She's still sitting in the same spot, but now she's looking around. It doesn't look like she's crying anymore."

"Okay, gang, let's go introduce ourselves so she won't feel so alone," Joy announced.

Joy led the way out the front door. Her short hair bounced as she walked. Aimee and Linda Jean followed behind her. I noticed how different we all looked from each other. Aimee's beautiful black curls were such a contrast to Linda Jean's straight brown hair. And I had my blond wavy hair pulled back in a ponytail.

We walked over to where the girl still sat on the curb. "Hi!" said Joy in her most cheerful voice. She handed the girl one of Abby's muffins. "We're your new neighbors."

We quickly introduced ourselves and told her about the neighborhood. I kept wondering if she was going to snap at us or run off. But she didn't.

Finally, her expression broke into a small smile. "It's nice to meet all of you. My name is Patricia Baker. Most people call me Tish, unless I'm in trouble or something."

"Okay, Tish it is then," I said, returning her smile. "Where did you move here from?"

Tish's eyes seemed to grow sad again for a minute. I thought she might cry.

"I'm kind of from everywhere. We move

around a lot because he is in the Air Force."
Tish pointed in her father's direction. "The
last place we lived was Lowery Air Force Base
in Denver. You know, that's where everyone
goes to ski."

"Wow," Aimee said. "That place sounds
exciting. We only get one or two tiny snowfalls
each year in Atlanta. And the only place around
here to ski is about three hours away. Do you
know how to ski?"

"I took a few lessons. I guess I was getting
pretty good at it, but I won't get to practice
anymore," Tish said sadly.

"Is Denver where your accent is from?" Joy
asked.

Tish grinned and tossed her shiny red hair
over one shoulder. "I always end up talking
the way the people do wherever we are. It drives
my parents crazy."

To prove her point, Tish stood up and
seemed to be preparing something in her head.
"Okay, pretty soon, I'll be talking like y'all,"
she said, mimicking our southern drawl. "I've
never heard an accent quite like the one y'all
have here in Georgia. It's really fun!"

We all laughed. "You're pretty good at that.
Can you do impressions of famous people?"

Aimee asked her.

Knowing Aimee as well as I do, I knew that she was already thinking of what talent Tish could bring to Party Time. I jabbed her lightly with my elbow to slow her down a little.

"Let's get to know her first before we put her to work," I whispered.

But Tish seemed pleased to have such an eager audience. "Oh, sure. I do lots of impressions. I can do almost any cartoon character you name."

For the next half an hour, Tish took on the voices of 10 cartoon characters from Saturday morning TV. It was amazing how she scrunched up her face to look like the characters, too. By the time she finished, we all were sprawled on my front lawn, listening to her cartoon character impressions. Tish was hilarious! Boy, were we lucky to have her move into our neighborhood.

"Hey, Tish," Joy said, when we all had stopped giggling. "It looks like your parents are going to be busy with the movers for a while. Why don't you come over to my house? There's this super club that we'd like to tell you about..."

# Two

A S I followed Joy into her house, I realized how natural it was for all of us to be there. Ever since we were little, Abby had watched us after school every day. We used to have so much fun playing games and building things. Now that we're 12, we spend our time planning our parties and helping Abby cook for her catering business.

Joy waited for all of us to file inside, and then she closed the door. "Hey, Abby," she called out toward the kitchen. "We brought someone over to meet you."

Abby waved from the kitchen door with her hand covered with flour. "Hi, everyone!" she greeted us.

"This is Tish. She's just moved into the neighborhood," Joy explained.

"Welcome, Tish. I'm Abby," she said. "I saw the moving van pull up earlier. You've all come over at just the right time, because I'm finishing up a batch of pizza pinwheels. They're great!"

"I didn't know you had any events planned for today," Joy said. "We would have been here to help."

"I got a last-second phone call from the Lamberts. They've decided to serve a whole meal at Jonathan's birthday party instead of just a snack. So, I'm in the middle of cooking-mania here. I'd love it if you'd like to pitch in."

Those were the magic words. Before Tish even had a chance to hear about The Forever Friends Club and our business, she was handed an apron and a hair net. She lined up behind us to wash her hands.

"Do you always cook like this?" Tish asked.

"Sure. We work for Abby's Catering," I told her as I stuffed my hair up under the net. "You don't have to do this if you don't want to. It's become a habit for us to pitch in whenever Abby is really busy."

"No, it's not that. It's just that I've never really cooked much before. My mom doesn't think that I'm old enough to cook."

"That's silly," I said. "Of course you're old enough. What grade are you in?"

"Eighth," she said.

"Me, too. But I'm not going to be 13 until next summer. I skipped a grade, so I really should be in seventh grade like these guys are."

I handed her the cheese grater and a hunk of mozzarella cheese. "Abby doesn't believe in food processors," I told her. "We do everything by hand. How about if you fill one bowl and I'll fill another with grated cheese?"

"Sure," Tish said. "This is going to be fun!"

I watched out of the corner of my eye as she turned the grater every which way trying to figure out how it worked. I guessed she wasn't kidding about never having cooked before. I stepped up beside her and set the flat grater across the top of the bowl.

After a few quick instructions, Tish was grating cheese as fast as I was.

"Be careful to watch out for your fingers when you get down to the end of the hunk of cheese," I warned her. "The grater is really sharp."

"I knew that," Tish snapped at me. I looked at her quickly to see what was wrong. "Uh, just ki-ki-kidding," she said, imitating another cartoon character.

"Hey, that's a terrific imitation," Abby said with a smile. "I'll bet the kids at your parties would really like that."

"We haven't had a chance to tell her about the club or the business yet," Joy told Abby.

"I'd like to hear about it," Tish said. "You said something about the club before when we were all outside."

"We're all a part of The Forever Friends Club," Aimee explained. "We all belong to it, and we have a few other members who don't come to meetings, but they do help us out at parties sometimes. We even have a member who lives in New York."

"New York? Parties? Meetings? I'm confused," Tish said. "You have a club, and you party a lot?"

"No," we all said at once, and then laughed.

"We give parties for little kids. We put together themes for the parties, and then we do the entertaining, the decorations, and sometimes the food, too," Linda Jean said.

"Yeah, and that's where Abby's Catering comes in," I added. "Our two businesses work together. But lots of Abby's accounts are for adult stuff that we don't do. We have the most fun when Party Time and Abby's Catering do parties together."

"We meet every day after school and give parties on weekends," Joy said as she rolled out a large rectangle of dough for the pizza pinwheels. "That way, the business doesn't affect our homework and school activities and stuff. Do you think you'd like to help us? You could see what your parents have to say about it."

Suddenly, a creepy shadow seemed to pass over Tish's face. Then, just as quickly, she smiled again. "No. My parents are hardly ever home. They really don't care where I go or what I do."

Tish stopped talking and went back to grating cheese.

"Does that mean you do want to be a member of The Forever Friends Club and Party Time?" I asked, thinking that Tish was a little strange. She didn't seem to be overly thrilled that we had invited her to join our club and our business.

"Sure, I'll join. What do I have to do?"

"First, we teach you how to make these pizza pinwheels," Linda Jean said. "They're our specialty. We make them for almost every party. Most people request them. Today, we're doing a relay-race party for Jonathan, a really cute six year old. Would you like to come and watch so you'll have a better idea of what we do?"

"I'd better not. I have a lot of stuff to put away in my room," Tish answered quickly.

I suddenly remembered that we'd practically kidnapped Tish. Her parents didn't even know where she was. They might even think that she ran away or that something terrible had happened to her.

"Shouldn't you call your parents or go over and tell them where you are?" I asked. My parents would have been panicked if I had just disappeared.

"Oh, don't worry. They won't be upset," Tish said with a bright smile. Her smile was cheerful, but it seemed like there was something that Tish was trying to hide from us. She wiped her hands on her apron and handed me her finished bowl of cheese.

"Okay, I'm ready for my pinwheel-baking lesson," Tish said.

I let Linda Jean lead the way. She's our expert pinwheel maker, especially since she created them. Actually, she created them by accidentally rolling pizza sauce onto the dough in place of cinnamon filling. The pinwheels have been our biggest seller ever since. She showed Tish how to spread the pizza sauce and the sausage filling across the thick dough. Tish took over and managed to spread the sauce pretty well, but she had a rough time getting the sausage filling on evenly.

"Spread it a little more to the left," I said. "The filling has to cover the dough completely, or the pinwheels turn out funny."

I sprinkled the cheese over the top of the mixture. For some reason, the pinwheels looked unusually clumpy. "They look like they have the measles," Joy teased.

"Or maybe freckles," Aimee added. "Giant brown freckles." She was referring to the cheese and sausage.

"Isn't that the kind Graham has?" I asked, poking fun at Aimee. I loved to tease her about Graham. She'd never admit how much she liked him, but she always defended anything anyone said against him.

"Graham doesn't have any freckles," she said. "And especially none as big as the one Tish is creating."

We enjoyed making fun of each other—that is, in a nice way. We never took things so far that we hurt someone's feelings. But I sensed that Tish didn't understand that we were just joking around. Her smile seemed forced. And it was especially weird that no one seemed to notice but me. My friends were all too busy finding new fascinating and disgusting ways to describe the mounds of sausage and cheese that Tish and I were spreading. Finally, it was time to roll up the dough and cut it into pinwheels. Linda Jean rolled up one end, and Tish rolled up the other.

"Make it looser," Aimee suggested.

"That's it. No, maybe a little bit tighter than that," Joy said.

"Okay, not quite so fast," Linda Jean instructed.

Suddenly, Tish yanked on the dough and put her hand right through the side of it. Joy started to crack a joke, but Tish stopped her.

"Just do it yourselves!" Tish shouted angrily. She tore the net off her hair and threw it on the kitchen floor. "I don't know what you need me for. You're all so perfect. You can just keep your club and keep your pizza pinwheels. I'm leaving!"

Tish was gone in a flash, and the slam of the front door echoed into the kitchen. We just stared at each other.

"What's her problem?" Aimee asked. "We were just kidding around."

Abby was still watching the doorway that Tish had run through. "I think you girls may have been a little hard on her. She only just met you. She probably wanted you to like her, and she thinks you were making fun of her. Maybe she's a little sensitive."

"Yeah, we probably scared her to death," I said. "We meet her and put her to work before she even gets to know us. She probably thinks we're pretty pushy."

"What should we do now?" Joy asked.

"How about if I go over to her house and tell her we're sorry?" I asked. "I could meet her parents, too, so they'll know who we are in case Tish does want to join our club. You guys can finish up the pinwheels. Okay?"

"All right, but tell Tish we didn't mean to pick on her," Aimee said.

"Okay. See you later," I called out and then closed the front door behind me.

I could have kicked myself for not being more sensitive to Tish's feelings. I should have realized that not everyone is as outgoing as the girls in our group are. But I would do my best to make it up to her. I really hoped that she'd still want to be a Forever Friends Club member. It would seem pretty strange to have a girl our age living nearby and not be her friend. It was important to me to make things right with Tish.

I thought about my sister, Kitty, as I walked down the street to Tish's house. Kitty and I used to fight a lot because we each felt like our parents liked the other kid better. We spent so much time picking on each other that we never took the time to get to know each other or have any fun together. It took a long time—too long, to be truthful—to finally tell each other how we felt. And once we did, everything worked out. It made me realize that honesty can solve just about anything.

I decided to approach Tish the same way. I would tell her how sorry we were for hurting her feelings.

As I stopped at the edge of her yard, I saw that Tish was helping to carry boxes into the house. I had never seen anyone work so quickly before. She marched one box after another down the ramp of the moving van and into the house. Her face looked determined as she walked by me. I knew that she saw me, but she didn't even look my way.

I walked closer to the van and touched her arm as she walked by me. What a mistake! Tish quickly dropped the box and whirled around.

"What do you want?" she demanded.

My heart was pounding. I had never met a girl like Tish before, that was for sure. I took a deep breath.

"I wanted to apologize for the way we all acted at Joy's house," I said softly. I didn't want to do anything that would make her any more angry than she already was. "We didn't mean to upset you."

In a split second, Tish's face changed from intense anger to a smile. "You didn't upset me," she said, tossing her red hair over her shoulder. "Come on, I'll show you my new room."

# Three

"TISH was really good about it," I told Aimee later that afternoon. We had arrived at Jonathan Lambert's house an hour early to set up everything for his party. Aimee and I had gotten busy setting the picnic table for dinner.

"Did she say what bothered her so much that she just ran out?" Aimee asked.

"No, she just said that there were no hard feelings. And then she didn't want to talk about it anymore," I told her. "She showed me around her new room. It's pretty big. And I met her mom. She seems nice. And that was it. I didn't ask her about the club again. I thought I'd let her think about it for a while."

Joy and Linda Jean came out of the house carrying all of the relay-race supplies.

"I still say Tish is a little strange," Aimee remarked. "I mean, one minute she's sweet, and the next she's sour. I wonder if she is that way all the time or if she just freaked out because it was moving day."

I finished decorating the table and walked over to help Joy arrange the large orange cones at the end of each lane for the relay races.

"Well, I know firsthand how tough moving day can be," Linda Jean said. "I remember how terrible I felt when my dad and I moved here. I snapped at my dad just about the whole way to Atlanta from California. I blamed him for moving us away from all my friends. And I was mad at my mom for divorcing both of us. I sure was a mess."

"Yeah, but when we came to meet you, you didn't yell at us and storm out of the room or anything," Joy pointed out. "I mean, you weren't weird to us."

"I did feel like being mean sometimes," Linda Jean admitted. "But I knew it wasn't your fault that I was upset."

"I guess everyone has a different way of coping with things," Aimee said. "I think we should give Tish another chance before we decide what she's really like."

All my friends are pretty terrific, but Aimee is especially great. Aimee is the one I turn to whenever I have a big problem and need advice. She always knows the right thing to say.

As a group, we all get along well, too. My mom says we have a mutual respect for each other that gets us through any petty arguments and disagreements that creep up from time to time. She also says that it's really unusual for four girls our age to be such close friends. I guess the normal thing for kids our age is to pair off into closer friendships. I'm really glad that we aren't like that.

"Well, I definitely think Tish would be a good addition to our parties. She could do a bunch of cartoon character imitations, and the kids would go wild," I said. "And you should've seen her whip the boxes out of the moving van and into her house. She works really fast."

"Well, we could use someone to help keep us organized," Joy suggested. "You know, to give us a push in the right direction to get things done. She could keep track of the parties and what supplies we need to buy."

"I wonder what she'd think about doing all that with us," Linda Jean said.

"It would be great if she wanted do it. And she could even do name tag duty," Joy said enthusiastically. "There are so many times when I practically run between writing up the last name tag and changing into my dancing outfit."

"Let's not get pushy again," Linda Jean said as she strung pieces of red, white, and blue crepe paper through the trees. The paper would indicate the finish line for the relay races. "Maybe we should invite Tish to some Forever Friends Club meetings first and see how she acts before we have her come to parties with us."

Aimee ran a long strip of crepe paper along the grass to mark the race lanes. "I agree with Linda Jean," she said. "I don't think Tish needs any more pressure. We should back off and offer her our friendship. It'll be up to her to decide if she wants to be friends with us or not."

"Yeah, and I guess we can't take a chance with Tish having a burst of anger during a kids' party," I said, even though I felt bad to say anything. "It would scare the kids for sure."

"And we could lose business," Joy pointed out. "Remember what happened when Aimee's father wanted to film us for his TV show? We were so nervous about being on camera that tons of things went wrong. And then people started canceling parties."

"I'm sure that's not going to happen if Tish helps us out," I assured them. "She seemed great when she showed me around her new house this morning. I think she'll be the perfect addition to our club. She just needs a little time to get adjusted."

After that, we had to hurry to finish setting up the table for the birthday presents before the first kids arrived. There were always one or two kids who came early, and we had to be ready for them.

The first boy to arrive was a cute blond dressed in little designer jeans. Joy rushed over to fill out his name tag, while I ran to the bathroom to change into my clown suit.

I decided to be a sports clown in honor of the relay-race birthday party. In place of my usual polka-dot suit, I wore baggy red sweatpants with three sets of colored leg warmers stacked on each leg. I borrowed the inflatable muscle shirt that Aimee's older brother, Randy, had worn for Halloween the year before. I even made up a banner to wear

31

across my chest that read, "Super Clown."

I was excited to see the kids' reactions to my new suit. I thought it was one of my most creative clown suits yet. As a hat, I wore an orange wig covered with layers of colorful headbands. I gave myself a last admiring look in the mirror and headed back to the party. As I walked into the backyard, Aimee was lining the boys up for the relay races.

"All right, you racers," Linda Jean called out. "Run down to the orange cones, and go around the cone at the end of your track and back to the beginning where you are now. The winner will receive a special prize. Just do your best, and have fun."

The four little boys who were racing looked determined. "Okay, GO!" Linda Jean yelled. Three of the boys stayed close together, and one pulled ahead. When Joy handed him his prize, a bright red stock car, he jumped up and down.

"Okay, gang," Joy called out. "Now I want you to watch me, and do what I do."

Joy loves being a ham and showing off her dancing ability. I don't think anything embarrasses her.

She took three graceful steps and then

leaped up into the air. Then she took three more steps and another leap. She continued until she reached the end of the course.

As Joy made her way down the course, 10 adorable six and seven year olds tried to imitate her. It was fun to watch the cute little boys as they tried to be dancers. As soon as everyone had finished practicing, Joy herded them back to the starting line.

"Now, remember," she said. "This time you don't win a prize for getting to the finish line first. You win a prize for trying your best. Okay, on your mark, get set, and go!"

The boys' attempts at ballet turned into absolute chaos. They flung their legs and arms all over the place! One boy toppled over, but he picked himself right back up and started again. They certainly weren't graceful, but they were having a great time.

I hurried to set up my magic tricks. I was on next. Then Aimee would take over at the crafts table and help the kids make their own party bags with first-place ribbons glued to the front. Linda Jean had brought along a snake with stripes that looked like racing stripes for the kids to touch. It was a great party.

In the middle of all the giggling, I couldn't help but think about Tish. Was Joy right about her? Was Tish really weird? Or was Aimee right when she said that everyone just copes differently? I didn't feel right saying anything to my friends since I'd stuck up for Tish. But I was worried that her temper tantrums might come back. One second she had been furious with us. And the next she was fine and didn't even want to tell us what we had said that was so wrong.

I pulled my thoughts back to the party. I love when the kids gather around to watch my magic act. "Okay, kids. I'm going to teach you a simple trick that makes people think you can wipe the smile on and off of your face. Watch."

I put my hand over my mouth and brought it up to my forehead. I smiled a big smile the whole time. Then I pulled it back down and made myself frown.

"Hey, that's cool," Jonathan said. "Let me try."

I picked him up and placed him on the table so that he could demonstrate his new skill to the audience. They clapped and clapped as each boy took a turn.

"Come back up here, Jonathan," I told him. "Now I'm going to teach you how to sew your fingers together."

He refused to budge. "No way. I'm not being sewn together."

"Relax," I said. "You don't use a real needle and thread for this trick. It's all make believe. Everything that magicians do is just make believe. That means that they make you think you are seeing something, but it's not really there. Let me show you what I mean."

One by one, I sewed my fingers together with an imaginary thread, pulling them together as I went. I tied the imaginary knot at the end and bit off the imaginary string. To the kids, the illusion looked real.

Suddenly, Tish's face flashed in my mind. She had seemed so happy to meet us that morning. And, when I had gone to her house to apologize, she seemed thrilled that I was there. But was that the real Tish? Or was the friendly Tish just make believe, an illusion that she created to fool us?

# Four

"I don't understand why Tish isn't here," I said on Monday as we were waiting to begin our daily meeting. "I'm sure that we told her that we have our meeting every day at Joy's right after school."

Linda Jean picked up her book bag and tossed it onto the dining room table. "Well, I guess I could get started with some homework if we're just going to sit around and wait for her," she said. I knew she was a little mad that we weren't doing anything. But my gut feeling was that Tish needed some friends, and I wanted to help her.

"We reminded her about the meeting during lunch," Joy said. "She said she would be here."

"Yeah, and she seemed really excited to be

included," Aimee added.

Joy opened the French doors that led into the kitchen. "Come on, let's have a snack. If Tish still isn't here by the time we're done, we'll just go ahead with the meeting."

"Okay," I said reluctantly.

"You know, Tish was great at lunch today. I think she was a riot," Aimee piped up. "She kept everybody laughing at all the cartoon characters she can imitate. She's really good—even good enough to be up on stage." Good old Aimee was reading my mind again. She knew that I really wanted to give Tish a fair chance.

"I hope she shows up," I said, sitting in my usual seat at Joy's huge kitchen table. "I wanted to talk more about what she could do for the party coming up this weekend."

Abby was off catering a meal for some meeting, but she had left us a snack to tide us over. She never let us go hungry—that was for sure! In the middle of the kitchen table was a heaping platter of tortilla chips and a crock full of cheesy nacho sauce. Aimee dipped a chip into the cheesy sauce and then sprinkled it with chopped olives, mushrooms, and shred-ded lettuce.

"I sure hope we did the right thing by inviting her to the party," Joy said.

"I'm sure we did. I'm sure Tish is over her tantrums. She's all moved in now," I told them. "So her life should start to get back to normal."

Joy took a long drink of soda. "I hope back to normal doesn't mean being late to meetings. We'll have to tell Tish how important it is to be on time for our daily meetings. That's our only way to keep everything organized." Just then, the phone rang. "And during our meetings, clients know that they can reach us to schedule parties," Joy said as she grabbed the phone.

"Maybe it's Tish calling to tell us why she's late," I offered.

We all watched as Joy answered and spoke to the person on the other end of the line. Joy cupped the phone and whispered, "It's Mrs. Curtis calling about Jaime's party on Saturday."

What a bummer! I was really hoping it was Tish calling with a perfectly good excuse about why she was late to the meeting. If she was much later, my friends were not going to be happy. And pretty soon they'd be mad at me.

I sighed and stuffed a handful of dry chips into my mouth. Why had Tish let us down? I couldn't decide if I was more mad or worried that something might have happened to her. What if something was wrong? We didn't even have her father's telephone number at the Air Force base to ask him if he knew where she was.

The sound of Joy hanging up the phone brought me out of my thoughts. "Mrs. Curtis said that Jaime finally picked a theme for her party. Are you ready for this? She wants a Disney World theme."

"Disney World? You mean as in rides and stuff?" Linda asked. "How can we do that?"

"No, not rides," Joy explained. "Jaime likes Disney characters. I guess she's the world's biggest fan of Micky Mouse and Donald and Daisy Duck. She loves just about any character from the Disney movies. Mrs. Curtis said Jaime would be thrilled with games and prizes that focus on the characters. It should be fun and pretty easy to do."

"Tish could do her impressions," Aimee suggested enthusiastically. "It'd be perfect! We'll make a list of cartoon characters, and she can choose the ones she wants to perform.

And how about if I help the kids make Mickey Mouse ears for our craft? I know how to make them out of painted paper plates."

"That's great, Aimee," Joy said. "I could create a dance to the music from one of the Disney movies."

In less than 10 minutes, we had talked through what my clown suit should look like, and which animals Linda Jean would borrow to introduce to the kids at our party. You see, Linda Jean used to have lots of different animals, but they had begun to take over her life and her house. Giving most of them to the retired people at Orchid Gardens Retirement Complex had turned out to be the perfect answer. The new owners didn't mind at all when Linda Jean asked to borrow the animals to bring along to our parties. And it was amazing how quickly Linda Jean had adjusted to living without her animals.

Next, we put together a list of possible prizes that the little girls would like. Mrs. Curtis was giving us some extra money to buy unusual items. After she'd jotted down gift number nine, Joy put down her pencil.

"Okay, gang, that was great," Joy said. "We're all set for Saturday."

I waited for someone to say it, but they didn't. Tish hadn't called, and she hadn't shown up for the meeting. I was mad and worried, but I didn't know what to do. Even if I did convince her to come to another meeting, I didn't know if my friends would want her there. But I really wanted to be there for Tish. I could sense there was some kind of hurt inside of her—the same kind of hurt that I used to feel whenever I thought Kitty got all of the attention and love from my parents.

I said good-bye to my friends and headed home. As I was walking up the sidewalk to my house, I turned to see the blue sports car driving down the street to Tish's house. I waved as they passed by. I saw Tish's dad wave back, but I couldn't see her mom or Tish very well.

I quickly bolted up the sidewalk, opened our front door, and ran inside to find my mom. I told her that I had to talk to Tish for a minute and ran back outside. I couldn't wait to tell Tish all about the cartoon theme for Jaime's party, and how much we wanted her to do her impressions for the kids.

They were getting out of the car when I reached their driveway. "Hello, I'm Krissy.

Wow, what a great uniform, Mr. Baker!"

"Why thank you, Krissy," Tish's dad said, smoothing the lapels on his blue Air Force dress uniform. "We've just been to a reception."

"Oh, he's much too modest, Krissy," Mrs. Baker said with a proud smile. I noticed that she was wearing another fancy business suit like the day they had arrived. I figured Tish's family must go to a lot of dinners and things. "This was my husband's welcoming party as the new base commander. He was recently promoted to full colonel, and this new job is very important to him. He gave a great speech, too. Didn't you think so, Patricia?"

"Hmm? Oh, yeah. It was great," Tish said from the backseat without any emotion. Tish's hair was the same shade of red as her mom's hair. They looked alike and talked alike. Mrs. Baker seemed really nice. I wondered why Tish was giving her such a mean look. After all, I could hardly be mad at her for going to hear her father speak. I think family things are really important. They come first for me, too.

Just then, a tall, skinny boy climbed out of the other side of the car. He didn't look a thing like Tish. He had dark brown hair and thick eyebrows. And he had the same smile that Tish's dad did.

"Hi," he said, leaning toward me to shake my hand. "Since it doesn't look like anyone is going to introduce us, I'll introduce myself. I'm Thomas Baker, Junior, but you can call me Toe. That's what my friends at college call me."

"Hi, Toe. That's kind of a different nickname. How did you get it?" I asked.

"Well, I hate to admit it, but I'm always tripping over my feet on the basketball court. I've learned to keep my sense of humor about it. The nickname Stub didn't exactly fit me, so my teammates started calling me Toe instead."

"That's pretty neat," I admitted. He seemed okay to me. "I like basketball, too. You'll have to meet Randy Lawrence, Aimee's older brother," I said, pointing to Aimee's house. "He's a basketball player for the high school. He's not as tall as you are, but he's a great player."

"I noticed the hoop attached to their garage," Toe said. "I'll have to go meet him while I'm home. Maybe we can shoot some baskets."

"I'm sure he'd like that," I said.

Tish yawned and started pulling clips out of her hair. Her hair had been done up in a soft bun with delicate ringlets around her face. "Why don't you ask Toe about the amazing three-point shot he made from the other end of the court?" Tish asked. "He can tell you all about how the shot just happened to win the game, too."

"That shot really was amazing," Tish's dad said with a big grin. "I can show you on videotape. Tom always sends us videotapes of his games."

"Uh, Krissy doesn't have time to watch it right now," Tish said quickly as she climbed out of the car. "She came over to talk to me about something." She smiled at me, but I could see the flash of anger in her eyes.

"Yeah, that's right, Colonel Baker," I said. "But I'd love to see the tapes later. Oh, and congratulations on your new job."

"Thank you, Krissy."

Tish's parents and her brother headed toward the house. Tish and I stood where we were until they were out of earshot.

"You don't have to be nice to them, you know," Tish said forcefully. "If you come over to see me, you can just ignore them, okay?

That's what I usually do. I ignore them, and they leave me alone. That's the way I like it."

"Why are you so mad at your parents?" I asked Tish. "They seem pretty nice to me. Your dad and brother both are very friendly. My dad and I watch sports together on the weekends if I'm not busy with parties. It's nice to spend time together."

"Well, I hate sports!" she barked at me. "And he's not my father. He's just my stepfather. Big deal!"

Whoa! So, Colonel Baker is Tish's stepfather! That could be part of the problem. I wondered how long he'd been married to Tish's mom. That can make a big difference. I remember how uncomfortable Linda Jean was around her stepfather, stepbrother, and stepsister until she got to know them. Even then, she was afraid she'd have to leave her father and move in with her mom and her new family. Luckily, none of that happened and everything turned out okay.

"That's hard," I sympathized. "Did they get married just before you moved here?" I thought about how tough it would be to adjust to a new dad, a new home, and a new school all at the same time.

Tish shook her head. "No, he and Mom got married when I was two. But I don't want to talk about it," she said as she led the way into her house and up the stairs to her room.

The whole thing seemed pretty strange to me. I thought that Tish definitely should be used to her family by now. But when she said she didn't want to talk about it, she wasn't kidding. Tish put on a big smile and pulled out her photo album. The pages were filled with snapshots of Tish and another girl with long blond hair and freckles.

"This is Carol, my best friend from Denver. We were so much alike. And we had so much fun together. We did practically everything together, and we stayed over at each other's houses a lot."

"She looks nice," I said, laughing at one picture of Tish and Carol having a water fight with hoses. "Who took this picture?"

"Toe did," she answered. "He can be okay sometimes."

"Do you miss Carol a lot? It must be hard to move away from your best friend. I know it would be awful if I had to leave Aimee, Linda Jean, and Joy."

Tish continued flipping the pages of her

album. "No, it's no big deal. Carol hasn't even written to me. She probably has a new best friend by now and has forgotten that I was ever there."

I looked at Tish's face to see if she was upset, but it was hard to tell. Her voice seemed strained like she was close to tears, but she kept a happy smile pasted on her face. It seemed like she was keeping a locked door on her heart and her feelings, and that they'd come bursting through the door at any second. Maybe I was exaggerating the whole thing. Maybe Tish was used to leaving friends behind. With her dad—I mean, stepdad—in the military, she was probably used to meeting new kids all the time.

There was a loud knock on Tish's bedroom door. As she opened the door, Tish's smile fell.

"Tish, we need your help for a few minutes. We're putting a few things up in the attic, and you're the smallest of all of us. Would you come and take them up there for us?" her stepfather asked.

"If I have to," Tish said, her lips pressed together.

"Oh, come on, Tish," I said, shrugging my shoulders at her stepfather. "The attics in these old houses are fun. I'm always crawling up the hole into ours to see what's up there."

I gave her a friendly nudge toward her bedroom door, and we followed her stepfather down the hallway. He led us to the master bedroom closet where there was an access to the attic. Toe was already there lifting the latch on the door and pulling down the fold-out attic stairs.

"If you'll go up, we'll hand you the winter stuff," her stepfather said.

Tish hesitated and folded her arms across her chest. She stared at the pile of skis, sleds, and snow saucers.

"Hey, I know. I'll go up first," I offered. "You can hand the stuff to Tish at the top of the stairs, and I'll take it from her and arrange it in the attic."

"That's a great idea, Krissy," her stepfather said. "It's nice to have someone who's familiar with these houses to help us out."

As I climbed the stairs, I wondered what Tish's problem was. Her stepfather and brother were really nice. Toe was great at telling jokes, and he seemed eager to be nice. Tish climbed up the stairs after me. But when I looked down at her, she wore a serious expression. It was like she refused to have any fun with her own family.

"Okay, are you ready up there?" Toe called.

"Yep, any time," I said.

"Here are the skis," he said, passing them one at a time to Tish, who then passed them to me.

"Here comes the sled," came her stepfather's muffled voice.

Tish huffed and puffed and groaned as she passed the sled over her head to me.

"It's heavy," she whined. "Why can't we do this later?"

"Because we want to get it done now," her stepfather said firmly. "There are only a few more things."

"I don't care," Tish said. "I'm tired and I don't want to do it anymore!"

"Lighten up, Tish," Toe said. "It's no big deal. Helping us for five more minutes of your precious time won't kill you."

I wondered if they were going to have a family fight right there in front of me?

"What do you care?" Tish shouted at Toe. "You don't have to live here! You have all your friends at college. You'll still get to ski and play in the snow."

"That's enough, Tish," her stepfather said softly. "Remember that you have a guest."

My stomach felt like it was in knots. I hated arguments of any kind. And this was even worse because I hardly even knew the Bakers. It was embarrassing to be involved in their problems. I took a deep breath of hot, stuffy attic air, and decided that I didn't want to be there for this.

"It's all your fault!" Tish continued, shouting at her stepdad as if I wasn't there. "You take everything and everyone away from me. And we'll never ever see snow again. Never!" I heard the plastic snow saucer clatter to the ground and the ladder shake as Tish stormed down it. She slammed the door on her way out. Then there was silence.

"Is she like that all the time, Dad?" I heard Toe whisper.

"I'm afraid she's like that too much of the time," he answered. "I just don't know what to do anymore."

"She wasn't that grouchy the last time I came home for a visit," Toe said.

Tish's stepfather sighed. "Well, Tish is so upset about this move. She blames me for taking her away from Carol. I have to tell you,

I don't like being the bad guy all the time."

"It's not your fault, Dad. No matter what she says."

"It's funny. I manage to solve the problems of an entire air force base full of men and women, but I'm at a loss when it comes to my own daughter."

I didn't know who I felt worse for, Tish or her stepfather. This was a mess, all right. I began to think that they'd forgotten about me. I stuck my head out of the opening.

"Hi!" I said softly. "If you want to pass the rest of the gear up, I'll finish putting it away."

Tish's stepfather and Toe both looked up at me with identical smiles. "I appreciate your help, Krissy," her stepfather said.

"You're welcome," I said. "And don't worry. I'm sure Tish will get over it."

"I hope so," he said and sighed. "I truly hope so."

# Five

I quickly finished stacking everything into the attic and said good-bye to Tish's step-dad and Toe. I just wanted to get away from all the tension. I had enjoyed seeing all of them, but I wasn't the one who could solve all their problems. From the sound of things, it seemed like there had been hostility and anger for a long time. It was just too bad that they hadn't worked things out before now.

I walked out of Tish's house and into the dim sunshine. I knew that across the street at my house my parents were busy fixing dinner like they did every day. My parents worked together at the phone company and seemed to enjoy it. My sister, Kitty, would be finishing up her homework at the kitchen table.

My daily routine was the same every day, too. But right now I didn't feel like doing much. I couldn't stop thinking about the argument between Tish and her stepfather. I wondered how she could hate him so much. And I was really disappointed that I hadn't had a chance to tell her about the cartoon theme party on Saturday. That would have cheered her up for sure.

"Hi, Kitty," I said as I walked into the living room. "How was school?"

"Cecily Boucher sailed an airplane out the window, and it landed in the principal's collar," she said proudly. I smiled, pushing thoughts of the Bakers to the back of my mind.

"Is this another one of your stories?" I asked with a grin.

"Nope, it's the truth," she said. "The principal didn't see it coming. She walked around with it in her collar until lunchtime. It was really funny."

"And then what happened?" I was waiting for the punch line. It was hard to tell when Kitty was telling the truth. She was such a great actress that she could fool me and everyone else whenever she wanted to.

"At lunch, Jeremy Weathers, a fourth

grader, asked her what that funny white thing was that was sticking out of her collar. The principal pulled it out, looked at it, and said very seriously, "Shhh, don't tell anyone, Jeremy, but this is a top-secret, miniaturized spy plane being tested by the United States government. Just pretend you didn't see a thing."

I was giggling by this time. The expressions on Kitty's face were hilarious. She must be so good at them from all that practice she gets trying to look excited about gross-tasting cereals for TV commercials. "So, what did Jeremy do?"

"You know Jeremy," she remarked. "He believed every word she said. The entire fifth grade class practically fell off their seats laughing."

"I'll bet you did." I carried my books to the dining room table where I always did my homework. We usually eat in the kitchen. "So, that really happened?" I asked casually.

"That's the truth. I promise," Kitty said, crossing her heart.

"Sure, Kitty. Sure."

Just then, Mom and Dad came into the living room carrying our dinner on trays.

"Do you need any help?" I asked.

"There are two more trays to bring in," Dad told me. "We thought we'd eat in here and talk about the three-day weekend coming up."

I nudged Kitty. "Come on. We'll each carry a tray."

With only a small protest, Kitty followed me to the kitchen. I was sure glad that we had worked out our differences a while back. For a little sister, Kitty was nice to have around.

Mom and Dad had filled our trays with steaming bowls of chili and hunks of home-made corn bread. Mom poured us large glasses of milk.

"Where are we going for the weekend?" Kitty asked.

"Well, that's what we wanted to talk to you two about," Mom remarked. "There are lots of places we could go that are fairly close to home. How about the Roosevelt Museum and the Little White House in Warm Springs? And there's Callaway Gardens. We could stay in a cabin and go hiking and exploring."

"How about that big amusement park near here?" Kitty suggested. "I want to try the Mind Bender Roller Coaster again. And Cecily says they have a super new secret ride that's

55

opening up next week."

"How does Cecily know all this?" Mom asked.

"Her dad helped design it," Kitty explained. "It goes over and around and up and down all at the same time."

"Oh, boy, I can't wait," I said, holding my stomach.

"We could go fishing on the Chattahoochee River," Dad offered. "That's much calmer than the Mind Bender."

"Yeah, that's for sure," I said, laughing. "Remember the last time we went to that amusement park? Dad and I had a contest to see who could go on the roller coaster the most times in a row without throwing up."

"Dad won as I recall," Mom said, joining in.

For the next hour we ate, talked, laughed, and finally decided to take the two-hour drive to Callaway Gardens, camp for two days, and then hit the amusement park on the way back. We all had a chance to talk and help make the decision. Everyone was looking forward to the trip. I realized then that my family was sure different from Tish's family. We made decisions together, and we really enjoyed being together.

The doorbell rang as we were clearing our dinner dishes. "I'll get it," I said, leaving my stack of dishes on the counter next to the sink.

I opened the door and found Tish standing on my porch. She had a big smile on her face and her hands behind her back.

"Are you okay?" I asked her. "Where did you go when you ran out earlier?"

"I'm fine," Tish said, ignoring my second question. "I brought you a present," she said, bringing her hands out in front of her.

"It's beautiful," I said, turning the ceramic vase over and over in my hands.

Tish looked down at her toes. "I made it at summer camp last year," she told me. "I want you to have it."

"Come on in," I invited her. "Let's talk." After I introduced Tish to my parents and sister, we went to my room. "Are you sure you're all right?" I asked again. "You were pretty mad earlier."

"Oh, don't mind my family," Tish said casually. "We yell all the time. It's the way we communicate."

"It didn't sound like communication to me. It sounded like you can't stand your step-father." I shook my head. "I sure don't understand why. He seems like a nice man to me."

"You're right," Tish said. "You don't understand. Let's just drop it, Krissy. I don't want to talk about him anymore."

I watched Tish as she nervously picked at her fingernails.

"What is this? Shrink week? Why are you staring at me? Are you trying to analyze me or something?" Tish asked self-consciously.

"No. I'm just trying to help a friend," I said.

"If you want to be my friend, you'll have to believe me when I tell you there is nothing wrong. If it makes you happy, I'll be sure not to yell in front of you again," Tish said.

"I do want to be your friend," I said softly.

"Good. Then it's settled," Tish crossed her arms in front of her and began looking around my room. "I think the vase would look good over there on your desk so the light from the window can make the colors glow."

I put the vase where she suggested, and then I changed the subject. "I didn't get a chance to tell you this afternoon, but Jaime Curtis' party is scheduled for Saturday. She wants the theme of her party to be Disney World. She loves all the Disney characters, and we'd like you to help us. That is, if you would like to help us."

Tish was grinning from ear to ear. "What do I get to do? What should I wear? When is it?" she asked eagerly.

"Slow down. One thing at a time," I laughed. I told her the details and gave her the list of characters we thought she might try to imitate.

"Wow. I have a bunch of hats from Disneyland that I got when we lived in southern California," Tish said. "You know, Mickey, Donald, Goofy, and Chip and Dale? I could switch hats and do the impressions that way. Do you think the kids would know who Chip and Dale are?"

"Of course, they would. Besides, Jaime wouldn't have asked for a Disney party if she wasn't really excited about it."

We planned and giggled and talked about the party until Tish had to go home to do her homework.

"Wow, I'm really glad to have you for a new best friend," Tish said as she left.

"Thanks...for the vase," I finally called after her. I couldn't believe how sometimes Tish was so easy to be around. I watched her walk toward her house, and I thought about those times when I couldn't understand her at all.

I know that talking about parties was a lot simpler than talking about problems. But being friends means doing a lot of both.

And Tish had just said that we were best friends. What would Aimee, Joy, and Linda Jean say about all of this? I knew it wouldn't be good. I was *their* best friend, wasn't I? For now, I just hoped that the Tish who came to the party on Saturday would be the same nice, cheerful girl I'd just spent two hours with. I didn't know what I would do if Tish the Terrible came instead.

# Six

"SHE'LL make it," I said. I had been glancing nervously at my watch for 25 minutes, hoping that I would be right. "Besides, it's not her fault," I said to Linda Jean. "Tish told me that her parents insisted that she have a fitting for her dress for Toe's graduation. And she wasn't too happy about it, either. You of all people should understand Tish's feelings about her stepfather."

"But Colonel Baker seems like such a nice man," Linda Jean protested.

"Louis is a nice guy, too," I reminded her. "But you couldn't stand him when he first married your mom. Remember?"

"Yeah, but you told me that Tish was only two when her mother remarried, and that she didn't even know her real father before Tish's stepfather came along. I was 12. That's a big difference."

"Maybe it's not to Tish," I defended her.

Abby had just started the car when I saw Tish walking down the street toward us. I let out the deep breath I'd been holding in. "We were just about to leave without you," Aimee told her as she climbed into the car.

"I'm really sorry. I told my parents that I had to be here, but as usual they just wouldn't listen," Tish explained.

I glanced at her. I wondered if she was already in one of her bad moods. It was hard to tell for sure. After all, her face was full of smiles as she pulled her cartoon character hats out of her tote bag. She seemed happy to be sharing all of this with us.

"Do you really think the kids will like my act?" she asked.

"I'm positive," Aimee said. She pulled a sample of her homemade Mickey Mouse ears out of her craft supply box. "Do you think you can teach the kids to say something simple with Mickey's voice, something to go along with the ears?"

"What about the Mickey Mouse Club song? You know, the one that goes, M-I-C-K-E-Y—

M-O-U-S-E, Mickey Mouse, Mickey Mouse..."
Tish sang the lyrics to the familiar tune in a squeaky Micky Mouse voice.

"Well, I didn't even think about that!" Aimee said. "You're going to be a great addition to Party Time. What are you doing on Saturdays for the rest of your life?"

"Gosh, I hope Party Time doesn't go on that long," Joy said. "I have some other things that I'd like to do with my life."

"Like what?" I teased. "Go back up to New York and dance with Russell again?"

"Oooh, Russell," Aimee said and put on a lovesick expression. She lifted her arms above her head to indicate a twirl like she was dancing the ballet with Russell. Russell is a ballet dancer with the New York Ballet. During our last Christmas break, we all went to New York to put on a birthday party for Alissa O'Toole, an actress who is our age. We had so much fun, and Joy even got to switch places with Alissa. Joy actually performed with the New York Ballet, and Russell had been her dance partner!

"Maybe," Joy said with a grin. "It might be nice to see him again."

"I didn't know you still thought about

Russell," Abby said. "He was a nice boy, wasn't he? I still can't believe that my daughter danced in a real ballet."

Just then, Abby pulled into Jaime Curtis' driveway and pushed the button on the outdoor intercom.

"Wow, this is a fancy place," Tish said as Mrs. Curtis spoke to Abby through an intercom system. Then, suddenly, the big iron gates swung open.

"Wait until you see the inside," I told her. "They have this carved marble staircase that goes up for three flights."

"The Curtises' home is on Atlanta's historical preservation list," Abby explained. "Their family has lived in Atlanta since before the Civil War."

Tish gazed up and down the long driveway. "Really? Did they own a plantation and grow cotton?"

"No, the Curtises don't do anything that Southern," Abby said with a grin. "I think they are pretty ordinary, except that Mrs. Curtis had a pirate or two in her family somewhere."

"Wow!" Aimee said. "Hey, pirates could be a great theme for a party. Kids always love treasure hunts and stuff."

"I believe the Curtises try to play down that side of their history," Abby said with a giggle.

"I wouldn't," Tish said. "If my ancestors were pirates, I'd tell the whole world about it."

"Do you know anything about what your ancestors did?" Linda Jean asked Tish.

"No way!" Tish said pretty loudly. "I don't even know what my real father did. And I'll probably never find out, either."

I decided not to say anything else to Tish. There was no use in upsetting her any more than I had already.

We concentrated on unloading our supplies and the food Abby had prepared. Parties were really easy when Abby's Catering and Party Time worked together. For today, Abby had made a neat Winnie the Pooh cake, and the bear even had a rounded belly and a little black nose.

Jaime and her mom met us in the driveway. Jaime was so cute. She had soft blond curls hanging halfway down her back and big brown eyes that stared cheerfully up at us. We had met her at a party the summer before when we did a dinosaur theme party for one of her friends. We were excited when Jaime's mom called us to do a party for her.

"Who's she?" Jaime asked, pointing her tiny finger at Tish.

Tish knelt down beside her and stuck a bright yellow duckbill on her head. "I'm Donald Duck," she said in a perfectly quacky imitation. "May I come to your—quack—party?"

Jaime giggled. "Did you bring Mickey and Daisy?"

"Quack. All your friends are in this bag, but shhh! Don't peek. They're sleeping," Tish whispered to her as if they were sharing a special secret.

"Come on," Jaime whispered back. "I'll show you where they can take their naps."

We followed Mrs. Curtis and Jaime into the recreation room. Abby set up the food while we started decorating. Having Abby to help us made everything go faster. We were ready for the party in plenty of time.

I felt like this party was going to be great. I decided I had been worried about Tish for nothing.

Everything sailed along just fine. The kids seemed to enjoy all of our acts, and Tish's impressions were a big success!

But then the catastrophe hit. I could sense it was coming just seconds before it happened.

All of the kids had left, and we were in the middle of cleaning up when Linda Jean went over to talk to Tish.

"Your act was really neat," Linda Jean complimented her. "Have you ever thought about imitating famous people as well as cartoons?"

"Nope," Tish said.

"Why not?" Linda Jean insisted. "I'll bet you'd be good at imitating people like presidents and famous actresses. Have you ever seen any old movies? I think those actors and actresses would be easy to imitate."

"Yeah, I've seen those movies, but I don't want to imitate people," Tish said in a loud voice. Then, she quickly forced her lips into a tight smile.

"I just don't see why not," Linda Jean said. "I mean, you're so good at voices and..."

Tish threw the rest of the garbage she was collecting into the trash with a thump. "Look. Do you really want to know why? It's because my stepfather does imitations of people. I don't want to be like him in any way. Now, are you satisfied?"

"Well, I think that's neat," Linda Jean said, ignoring my silent looks that were telling her to cool it. I wanted to tell her to drop it. I knew

Tish was going to blow. "You and your step-dad should perform together sometime. Maybe it would help you to get to know him better."

"What do you know about it?" Tish raised her voice another notch. "There's no way I'll ever perform or do anything else with my stepfather."

"Why don't we finish this discussion out-side?" I suggested quietly. Mrs. Curtis and Jaime had gone to put her gifts away, but they could be back at any moment.

At this point, Tish and Linda Jean were standing nose to nose, completely unaware that the rest of us were watching them.

"Tish Baker, I happen to know a lot about learning to get along with a stepfather, be-cause I have one, too. And I know that never talking and never doing anything together isn't the answer. Maybe he isn't perfect, but you have to give him a chance," Linda Jean encouraged.

Then Tish said, "I don't want to give him a chance. For 10 years all he's done is mess up my life. I don't want to hear any of your stupid ideas. They won't work."

"No, they won't—unless you give them a try," Linda Jean told her. "Why don't you do something to solve your problem?"

That was the last straw. Tish stormed out of the recreation room and left us all staring after her.

"Why did you pick a fight with her like that?" I accused. "Everything was going well until you started talking about her stepfather."

Linda Jean turned to me, and the anger from her fight with Tish was still strong in her eyes. "All I did was ask her about imitating people. How was I supposed to know her stepfather did impressions of people, too?"

"There's no way you could have known," Aimee said, coming up and putting an arm around Linda Jean. "But you were a little hard on her, Linda Jean."

"I think it's Tish's fault," Joy added. "She flew into that stupid rage over pinwheels. Then she didn't tell us she had to skip our meeting. And now this. I don't think we should invite her to help us anymore. Once is enough."

We finished cleaning up, and Aimee picked up her craft box and started for the door. "We were lucky this time. The party was over before Tish blew up. Next time it might be right in the middle of the party."

"You don't know that," I said in Tish's defense. I grabbed my clown bag and followed Aimee out the front door. "Besides, what about giving Tish another chance? That's what you told her to do with her stepfather."

When no one said anything, I continued. "I just don't believe you guys," I said in disgust. "Tish needs our help now, and you're turning your backs on her. We helped Graham when he had a problem, didn't we? And we helped Alissa O'Toole, too. Why not Tish?"

I knew that I might be pushing my friends too far this time. I wondered why I was sticking up for this girl who I barely knew. For some crazy reason, I felt that I was the only one who could fight Tish's battles for her.

Joy stepped up beside me. "Maybe what Linda Jean said needed to be said," she pointed out. "Tish can't go on forever without talking to her stepdad about their problems. Maybe it's time someone told her to shape up."

Jaime and her mom came to the front door to wave good-bye to us. Jaime ran after us and gave us each a big hug of thanks.

"Tell Tish good-bye," Jaime said as we left.

"I will," I told her.

Tish was waiting in the car for us. She had

her head turned so that she wouldn't have to look at us.

"I don't care how much it needed to be said," I whispered to Joy before we got into the car. "I don't think hurting someone's feelings is the best way to help."

# Seven

THE ride home after the party was tense, and everyone was quiet. It felt like we were sinking deeper and deeper into a fog of hurt feelings. Today had been so far from our fantasy about a new girl moving into our neighborhood. We had wanted her to become an instant member of our club and to like everything that we liked. Maybe we had just wanted too much too soon.

I had hoped that our regular meeting on Monday would set things right again. But it didn't. Tish wasn't invited. And Joy, Linda Jean, and Aimee all kept up a disgustingly cheerful discussion about things that didn't seem to matter. I was ready to scream.

I tried three times to bring up the subject of Tish and what had happened on Saturday.

I wanted to solve the problem right then and there. But while my friends didn't seem to be blaming me for Tish's outburst, they weren't being overly friendly to me, either. They quickly changed the subject away from Tish whenever I mentioned her. I was relieved when I glanced out the window and saw my parents' car drive up our driveway.

I quickly mumbled good-bye and ran home to have a long talk with my mom. I definitely needed some good advice. But as soon as dinner was over, Mom rushed off to a baby shower that was being given for her secretary. And Dad left to drive Kitty to a rehearsal for a commercial she was starring in on Saturday.

I plopped down on the couch to think. There had to be an answer to all this. I was usually the organized one of our group. It seemed like everyone always came to me with questions. And here I was all alone, and I couldn't come up with a way to help Tish or myself.

I walked over and sat down in our living room window seat. I picked up my newest novel about a girl who falls for a cute new guy in school, but her best friend hates him. I felt like I could relate to that confusion.

From the corner of my eye, I saw someone walking. I glanced up in time to see Toe walking past our house. I knew that was the answer! I scribbled a quick note to my parents to tell them where I went and ran out the front door. I finally caught up with Toe at the corner.

"Hi," I said. "Boy, you sure walk fast. Are you walking to keep in shape for basketball?"

"I usually jog, but tonight I just felt like walking. I wanted to get away from all the craziness going on at home," Toe admitted.

"What craziness?" I asked, hoping he wouldn't think that I was being nosy. I mean, I was stuck in the middle when they were yelling before. And they didn't seem too embarrassed then.

"Oh, it's nothing really. I shouldn't have said anything."

"Do you mind if I walk with you?" I asked. "No one's home at my house. It'd be nice to have some company."

"No problem. But I have to warn you that I'm walking five miles. Can you handle that?" Toe asked, looking down at my untied tennis shoes.

"Of course, I can," I said with a grin. I squatted down to tie my laces, and then we were off. I was almost running to keep up with Toe's long strides, but I was determined to find a way to talk with him about Tish. I decided the direct approach was the only way.

"Toe, could I talk to you about Tish? It's really important," I said.

"Yeah, sure," Toe said hesitantly. He probably had a good idea of what I wanted to ask him. "Is Tish giving you a hard time?" he asked.

"Actually, I think Tish gives herself a hard time," I said. "She always seems so angry. I've been trying to think of a way to help her. I have tried to show her that I want to be her friend, but that doesn't seem to be enough."

"Tish and my father, as you know by now, don't get along very well," Toe said. "They used to, but this last move really upset Tish. She had to leave behind the best friend she's ever had. She and Carol did everything together. She used to spend weekends with Carol's family going skiing. She really misses having someone there all the time to do things with."

"And she blames your father for taking that away from her?"

"Exactly. She resents the fact that Dad is in the Air Force, and that he is transferred every three years or so. And this time it was Dad's choice to move. He had enough tenure in Denver to retire, but he wanted this promotion and to work for a few more years."

"He's still really young," I said. "I don't blame him for wanting to keep working. He's just trying to make a better life for his family, right?"

"Tish doesn't see it that way," Toe said.

"Can't you talk to her about her feelings?" I asked eagerly.

Toe shook his head. "I've tried, Krissy. I really have. But she keeps insisting that nothing is wrong. She's either sweet and pretends that everything is great, or she's running off in a huff. There doesn't seem to be any middle ground with her."

"That's the way she's been with me, too. All my friends are already fed up with her. They don't want her to come to our parties or our meetings that we have after school every day. They're all afraid that she'll have another tantrum. We're not used to girls who act that way."

We turned the corner, and the cool breeze whipped through my hair as we walked across the vacant field at the end of the street. I was breathing hard, but it felt good to wear off some of my tension.

"It's too bad that Tish couldn't jog or walk to get rid of some of her anger," I said.

"There are lots of things she could do to calm herself down. At the top of the list is trying to understand Dad's point of view. I know she's only 12, but she should realize that Dad had a tough decision to make," Toe said thoughtfully. "But besides that, Tish could do other things like make an effort to make new friends. She could get involved in school sports to get some exercise."

"Do you mind if I ask what happened tonight?"

"No, I don't," Toe said and then was quiet for a minute. "I think Tish is pretty lucky to have met you, Krissy," he said with a smile. "It sounds like she's been tough on you already, but you still care."

I didn't say anything. I waited for Toe to continue. "After dinner, things around the house started getting crazy again. Tish was slamming doors and making a big fuss over something. I don't even know what the problem was, but I just couldn't handle it anymore."

"I'm sorry for making you talk about it," I said softly.

"Talking about it isn't hard," Toe said. "I just wish that Tish could talk or walk it out of her system. I really love my little sister, you know. I wish I could be around to try to help her. But I have to go back to college next week."

We talked for another hour about ways we could help Tish to cope better. I was glad that I'd scribbled that note before leaving my house. My parents would have been worried sick if they didn't know where I was for so long. Finally, we were back at my house.

"Well, you made it the full five miles. How do you feel?" Toe asked me.

"I feel fine now, but I may be a little sore in the morning. I'm glad we had a chance to talk," I told him. "Thanks. It was fun."

"I don't know how much help I've been. But I do know that activity is the key to working through problems, Krissy. If Tish could get involved with your group and join some school activities as an outlet for her energy, she'd be much better off. And she needs a special friend to talk to—someone to give her good ideas for coping with problems."

"Like counting to 10 before you speak or

run off?" I suggested.

"Exactly. And anything else creative that you can come up with," Toe said. "Like wearing out your tennis shoes by trooping around the block."

I laughed and looked at the bottom of my shoes. "Yep, they're practically steaming."

Toe laughed, too. He licked his finger and touched the bottom of my shoe. "Ssss," he said, making a sizzling sound.

We said good-bye, and I watched Toe head off down the street. "The only trouble I'm going to have," I mumbled to myself after he had gone, "is getting Tish to admit she needs some help in the first place."

I finished my homework, then gave each of my parents a kiss good night. It had been a long day, and I couldn't wait to crawl under the covers.

But at 3:00 in the morning, I sat straight up in bed. I heard the chime of the antique grandfather clock in the dining room. I couldn't get thoughts of Tish out of my mind. How could I get her to see how nice her parents really were? And how was I going to convince my friends to give Tish a third chance?

By the time I got out of bed the next

morning, I had made up my mind. I decided to spend some time with Tish. Maybe if she got to know me better—and learned to trust me—she would open up about what she was really feeling inside. I just hoped that my friends would understand.

* * * * *

"We haven't seen much of you this week," Joy said to me on Friday. We were helping Abby cater a dinner for a garden club party.

I tied my blue "Abby's Catering" apron tightly around my waist and secured the net around my hair. Wearing a bun on top of my head is the easiest way to control my long hair.

"I've been doing a few things with Tish and walking in the evenings with Toe," I told them. "I can go five miles in an hour now."

"That's pretty good," Linda Jean said. "But isn't he a little old for you?"

"Of course, he's too old for me," I said, looking at her strangely. "We're just friends!"

"Toe and Krissy, sitting in a tree, K-I-S- . . ." Aimee began.

"Oh, grow up!" I said, turning away from her to stir the sauce over the meatballs.

"Touchy, touchy," Joy said. "But then you did say you hung around with Tish this week. I guess that explains your short temper."

"I think that's quite enough, girls," Abby said. "Let's enjoy the party, okay?"

"Yes, we have more important things to worry about," Linda Jean said anxiously. "The crock pot is going crazy and oozing drips of cheese dip all over the tablecloth."

Abby rushed to her side and quickly lifted the lid off the boiling pot. A large blop of cheese exploded onto the white linen cloth.

"Get the sponge, Joy," Abby ordered. "Unplug the cord, Krissy." She held the lid down on the pot until the heat subsided.

"Thank you, girls," Abby said. "A little bleach water in that spray bottle over there should take care of the spill. Aimee, hurry to the kitchen and bring out a large platter for the tortilla chips. We'll ladle the sauce over them and make instant nachos. Krissy, bring that extra bowl of strawberries over here and set them in the empty spot. There," she said, wiping off her hands as we all scrambled to do everything that she'd asked. "The problem is solved, and the guests aren't due to arrive for two whole minutes."

I thought about Tish, and how she would have handled the cheese mess. She probably would have had a fit and left. But Abby was so different. She seemed to come to life during crazy moments. She loved fixing problems and solving things. It was like a game to her.

I guess I was kind of like Abby. I always had a list of everything that needed to be done. I had never really thought about it, but I wondered what other people did to stay calm.

Then I turned my attention back to the party. The garden club was hosting a fancy fund-raiser for a visiting politician. Some of Atlanta's richest citizens were coming to give their support. And Aimee's father would be there to interview the politician.

As the dinner got underway, I realized that being rich doesn't necessarily make you happy, because some of the people were very rude. Joy was having trouble with a man at the far end of the room.

"Little girl," he called out to her. "I really must insist that you pour some of that brandy over my fruit."

"I'm sorry, sir. I can't do that. I'm under age, and I'm not allowed to serve alcohol," Joy said politely.

"Why are you working here if you are under age?" the man snapped at her. "Why are we being served by children?" I could tell that he was slurring his words. I thought he might be drunk.

Joy's hands clenched and unclenched by her sides. Even from a distance, I could see she was holding back tears. "My mother is the caterer," she finally managed to say. "I'll get her to pour your brandy if you'd like."

"No one's going to know if you pour it," the man said. "Just hand the bottle of brandy to me. I'll take it from there."

The rest of us weren't supposed to leave our posts, so I waved frantically at Abby. She was busy serving trays of hors d'oeuvres to the guests of honor.

"Hey, Abby," I finally called out. When she looked up, I pointed to the man who was hassling Joy.

But when I looked at Joy's face, I realized that she was handling the whole thing pretty well. She was upset, but she could handle it. She wasn't going to explode or lose control. She was not going to yell at the man even though he might deserve it.

"I'm sorry, sir. If I break the law, I will lose

my job. And I do have a special work permit, so it's fine that I'm serving here tonight. My mother is on her way over now, and I would be happy to introduce you to her. She can pour your brandy for you. What is your name, sir?"

"Oh, just forget it!" he snapped. We watched him salute Abby as he walked past her. "Fine group of youngsters you have working for you," he remarked.

"Thank you," Abby replied. "We do our best." We were all holding back giggles as the man walked out of the club. "Okay, so what was that all about?"

"Don't worry, Abby," I said. "Joy has everything perfectly under control."

Abby smiled at her daughter. "Of course, she does. But I'm sorry that I brought you girls to this dinner. Some of these people are pretty difficult. And I didn't realize how much drinking there would be. If you have any more trouble, just signal for me."

The rest of the evening went pretty smoothly. As we cleaned up afterward, I thought about how each person has a different boiling point. Some people react quickly, and others take a long time to think things through before saying anything.

For me, walking and reading help to keep me calm. Joy dances away her problems. Aimee loses herself in a crafts project, or she plays with her little brothers. And Linda Jean plays with her animals or creates crazy science experiments.

Now, if only I could figure out what Tish Baker could do to let off steam, things would be great. But even if I did have the perfect answer, how would I ever get Tish to listen to me?

# *Eight*

I observed Tish all week as we did things to-gether. I realized that the one thing she really likes to do is go shopping. She rarely buys anything. She just likes to try on clothes—and mostly weird combinations that make her look like a different person!

I thought about ways to convince Aimee, Linda Jean, and Joy to come with us to the mall. But every time I mentioned Tish, they ignored me. So, I gave up talking about her.

Tish and I did have fun times together. When she was away from her family, she could be really funny when she wanted to be. We pointed to all the cute boys we saw walk by and giggled when they saw us staring at them. We loved to sit in the center eatery section of the mall and snack on a huge pizza topped with barbecued chicken and cheese. If only there weren't the angry times, too.

On Saturday, we didn't have a single party booked. I was thrilled. It had been ages since we'd had a free Saturday.

"What do you want to do?" Joy asked us. We were sprawled around her living room. "I hear that the Atlanta Ballet is doing *Still Point*."

"Isn't the Piedmont Arts Festival going on this weekend at the park?" Linda Jean asked.

"No, it doesn't start until next weekend," Aimee said. "Did you guys know that I'm displaying a couple of my sculptures at the festival this year?"

"I didn't," I said. "That's great, Aimee."

"And did you know that I'm dancing a solo dance for our big recital next Sunday?" Joy asked.

"I didn't know that, either," I mumbled. "Boy, I guess we haven't had a chance to talk much lately. We're so busy scheduling and working at parties that we hardly have time to catch up with each other anymore."

"It's not that bad," Joy replied. "I just forgot to tell you."

"We used to go to all of your performances,"

I recalled. "Now, it seems like we're all too busy."

"Why don't we go to the mall?" Linda Jean suggested eagerly. "There's a great jewelry sale going on at the Beautiful Lady store in Lenox Square. It's half off the clearance stuff."

"That sounds like fun," Aimee said. "I've been wanting some new hair clips to go with the new tie-dye outfit I just made."

"What outfit?" I asked.

"Oh, it's a neat shorts set I made a couple of weeks ago. I'll wear it to the mall, okay? I'm sure my brother Randy would drive us. He just got his driver's license, and he'd be excited to take us anywhere."

Suddenly, I had an absolutely perfect idea. "I have something to do before I go to the mall. How about if I meet you at Lenox Square in a little while. I'm sure Dad will drive me there. Okay?"

"Okay, how about in two hours in front of the Milk Shake Shack?" Joy asked.

"Sounds great! See you then," I said as I walked out Joy's front door.

What I needed now was some good luck. I hurried to my house to make sure Dad could drive me to the mall before I put the second part of my plan into action.

As soon as he nodded yes, I ran to the phone and called Tish. I knew that I was taking a real chance by inviting her to go with me. The Forever Friends might be really mad at me for tricking them. But knowing my friends as well as I did, I just couldn't believe that they'd turn away from Tish if she really needed their help.

Dad dropped us off near the main mall entrance about an hour later. We headed for Tish's favorite clothing store.

"So, Tish," I said as we browsed. "It has been a pretty good week, huh? We've had fun doing stuff together."

"Yeah, Krissy. It's been the best," Tish said. "It's really neat having a best friend again."

"I'd also like you to get to know Aimee, Linda Jean, and Joy, too. They're still my friends, too."

"I know. Maybe next week." Then she held up a pair of shoes for my opinion. "What do you think of these shoes? Aren't they the dumbest things you've ever seen? That strap would probably cut off your baby toe!"

Tish was great at changing the subject when she didn't want to talk about something. We had spent a lot of time together last week, but every time I tried to bring up the subject of her parents, she managed to change the subject. And I was afraid to push her too hard.

I noticed that talking about clothes was Tish's favorite way to change the subject. She and Carol, her former best friend, had loved to put together crazy outfits.

I looked both ways as we rode the escalator down to the lower floor of the store. We were supposed to meet the gang in about half an hour, and I still had to find a way to tell Tish what I was up to.

As I held up a shirt in front of the mirror, I saw Aimee, Linda Jean, and Joy in the mirror's reflection. They were looking at the jewelry across the aisle, but I couldn't take a chance that they would spot us, too.

"Oops," I whispered frantically. I ducked down before they could see us. "I think I lost a quarter."

Tish bent down to feel around beneath the racks of clothing. I faintly heard Joy's voice as they walked by.

"I'm sure that I saw her on the escalator," Joy said.

"Well, I don't see her," Aimee said.

"Okay, we'll just meet her when we planned to," Joy said. "Maybe I'm seeing things."

I looked over at Tish, and she didn't seem to be paying any attention to Joy. I was relieved that Joy hadn't said my name. "Here, I found it," I said, putting the imaginary coin in my pocket and standing up. As soon as I was sure my friends were gone, I led Tish into a dressing room. I wanted to be safe just in case Joy came back for another look around.

"Hey, you'd look great in this," I said, handing her a jumpsuit and lightly pushing her through the door.

"I'll give it a try," she said.

"How about getting something to drink before we try on any more stuff?" I asked through her dressing room door.

"Sure," she said. "But let me show you this outfit. It's great!" She opened the swinging door wide and paraded in front of me in a wild, zebra-striped jumpsuit. It had red splashes all over it as if someone had gone wild with a paintbrush.

I almost choked from laughing so hard.

"It's me, don't you think?" Tish asked with a grin.

"Well..." I hesitated. I wondered if I should tell her the truth.

"Get real," Tish said, laughing at the

worried expression on my face. "It makes me look like a zebra with the chicken pox. I didn't expect you to say yes."

"So, what *is* your style?" I asked her a few minutes later as we slid into a booth near the back of the Hamburger Stop.

"Actually, I like pretty crazy combinations. But my parents won't let me wear wild stuff."

"Really?" I asked.

"Yeah, my parents would think I'd gone bonkers or something if I came home with a zebra outfit," Tish said.

I looked up just as Tish's face seemed to cloud over. "Well, I guess they really wouldn't care whether I bought weird stuff or not," Tish said in an irritated tone of voice. "They don't care much about what I do or where I go."

That was the opening I'd been waiting to hear. "Tish, why do you feel that way?" I asked softly. "When I was at your house, I thought your parents seemed to care about you a lot. When you went flying out of the bedroom that day we were loading up the attic, your step-father was very upset about it. He said he didn't know what he could do to make you feel better."

"Really?" Tish asked. For a minute she

seemed amazed, almost curious about her stepfather's reaction to her tantrum. Then the mask dropped back down. "He could move us back to Denver," she shot back, anger sparkling in her eyes. She started to stand up.

"Please don't go, Tish. I'd really like to help you." I put my hand on her hand and held her angry stare.

"How do you want to help, Krissy? The same way your friends helped me at that party? By telling me what to do with my life? Everyone is always telling me what to do. I feel like I've never been allowed to make one decision on my own in my whole life!"

"Except when you decide to walk out on something or someone," I said. I sipped my drink and waited while she calmed down and sat down again. I just sat there quietly waiting for Tish to say something.

"I don't know what to do, either," she said, her voice barely above a whisper. "I try so hard to control myself. They make me so mad. Really mad. I keep it in for as long as I can. And then I can't stand it. I just explode."

"Like with the pizza pinwheels?" I asked. Tish nodded and tore at the side of her paper cup. "And with the skis and the attic?"

"You don't understand, Krissy," Tish said. "He takes everything away from me. And I'm just supposed to go along with things because he thinks I'm so young. It's because of him that we always have to move. My mom accepts it and doesn't seem to care. But I do. I've lost my friends and my school. I can't even go skiing anymore, and I was getting good at it."

"But there are things you can do here in Atlanta, too. You can help us out at our parties and come to our Forever Friends Club meetings and go skating and sightseeing. I think you're lucky to be able to move to different places. I've lived on this same street all of my life. And I've only been to Hollywood and New York."

"I did try to come to your meetings, Krissy, but my stepfather always has something for us to do. It's always him, him, him. And when we're not going to his military stuff, all my parents talk about are Toe's college awards and his basketball games. I feel like I don't even matter."

I sighed. She sounded just like I did before Kitty and I worked things out. "Tish, you know in your heart that that's not true. You care a lot about them, or you wouldn't get so angry.

And I saw how much they care about you, too."

"Then why do they treat me like such a baby?" she asked as she pounded the table with her fist. "Why don't they think about what I want?"

I took a deep breath. "Maybe because you act like a baby sometimes," I said. Her eyes flashed at me. "Sometimes I act like a baby, too."

I could tell she was about to get up and leave. "Now hold on for a minute." I proceeded to tell Tish about my jealousy over Kitty's modeling jobs, and about how I nearly wore myself out trying to be perfect so my parents would notice me, too.

"After a while, I realized that they knew I was there all along. But I was stuck in my own problems and couldn't even see things clearly. Once I took the time to talk to Kitty and to my parents, it was amazing how easy it was to work things out."

"You think I should talk to them? I don't know," Tish said.

"I'm saying you should try to stay and talk things over when the conversation gets tough instead of running away from it. You might find out what is really bothering them and what is really bothering you."

"I just wish they would do what I want once in a while," Tish complained.

"Are you sure they know what that is?"

After a couple of minutes, Tish smiled. "All right. I get your point," Tish said.

"Hey, there," Aimee called out to us as they walked down the aisle between the booths. "The conversation sounds serious back here. We wondered what happened to you, Krissy, and then we decided to get a drink. What a coincidence that you are here, too."

"Yeah, we hope you don't mind if we intrude," Linda Jean said. "We couldn't help but hear the last part of your talk. What's the deep discussion for?"

Tish looked nervous, as if she might run off again. I jumped in before she had the chance.

"Tish and I were just talking about things you can do to solve problems, like talking things over with your parents. Tish wants to deal with her anger better and to get her problems out so that she can solve them. I was telling her some ways to relax when things aren't going well. Like Joy did the other night when that man was bothering her about being so young. She kept her cool and solved the problem. Tell Tish about it," I urged.

"You should have seen him," Joy began. "He ordered me to serve him liquor. I can't do that because I'm under age, but he wouldn't accept that."

"What did you do?" Tish asked.

"I counted to 10 and then told him about the state law. Then I counted to 10 again. It seems like I did that 20 times."

"I've tried that, but it doesn't work for me," Tish said thoughtfully. "I get to 10 and I'm still mad. And even when I get up to 20, I still don't cool down."

"Have you tried counting to 100?" Aimee asked, and we all laughed.

"Hey, I'm serious," Joy insisted. "Sometimes I sing a cheery song in my head so I won't think about what's really going on. Or I picture the dance steps to my favorite ballet."

"Does it work?" Aimee asked. "I have to actually sit down and physically work on a project to get my mind off my troubles. Remember when I was having all that trouble with Graham? Sometimes the only thing that kept me sane was crocheting. When all that stuff was going on, I almost finished a whole bedspread."

"Wow!" Tish exclaimed. "It sounds as if you get as mad as I do."

"Well, I have four brothers," Aimee told her. "So, there's a lot of opportunity for it!"

"Well, I only have one sister, but she makes me mad enough all by herself," I said. "She's always borrowing my clothes. She thinks she's big enough to wear them. So, guess what I did? I made a system of stickers so I can tell which pieces of clothing are missing."

The waitress came around and took new orders for everyone. And as we talked, Tish slowly relaxed. Each one of us told stories about how the people in our families bugged us, or about things we had to deal with. Linda Jean told Tish about having to give up most of her pets. And I told her how I used to be a part of every club in school because I wanted to be perfect—the way I thought Kitty was.

Then, suddenly, I noticed that Tish had gotten very quiet. "So, will you let us help you with your problems? You can come to us when things are bothering you," I said.

"What problems?" she asked quickly. "I don't have anything to talk about."

"You have to be kidding," I said. "Nothing that we've said today means anything to you? You just said a few minutes ago that you get really angry sometimes. We're here to help you come up with ways to make you feel better." I was getting really angry myself.

Then Tish grinned. "Maybe you'd better count to 10, Krissy," Tish said with a giggle. "This time I was only joking!"

# *Nine*

OUR shopping trip turned out to be more talking than shopping. I had been so mad at Tish that it took me a few minutes to calm down from her joke. But after that, she opened up a lot and told us her frustrations about leaving Carol behind and not feeling as perfect as her brother is.

Tish even decided on a few ways to try to control her anger. She even promised us that she would talk with her parents about her feelings. She was going to write down everything that she wanted to say to them. And when they talked, Tish agreed to stick to her list. That way, she wouldn't jump off the subject or run away because she was mad. And, if she chickened out at the last minute, she could hand them her list. I figured that the list alone would tell them a lot about what Tish had been feeling.

Tish also agreed to start an aerobics class at the health club that her parents had just joined. They had a special program for teens and pre-teens that combined dancing and exercising. Joy had suggested that Tish consider a ballet class, but Tish didn't think she would like it.

"We have a family membership to the health club. I guess I should use it, too," she had pointed out.

We all told her that we needed her in the Forever Friends Club and Party Time.

"But what about times when little things go wrong?" Tish asked nervously. "I can try really hard to be calm, but I don't always know for sure if I can. I mean, what if I yell at a kid or something?"

"Usually one of us can tell when you're getting mad," I said.

"How?"

"You get a certain look in your eyes," Joy said, remembering.

"Yeah, you kind of stiffen up and paste a huge fake smile on your face," Aimee added.

"Then you start talking really fast," Linda

Jean explained and smiled.

"Wow, I didn't know I did all of those things," Tish said.

"How about if we give you some sort of signal as a warning?" I suggested. "We could wink, jump up and down, or wave a flag at you."

"Or you could slug me in the arm," Tish suggested with a giggle.

"Well," I said. "I'm sure a wink would be enough if you promise to react to our signal and try to calm yourself down."

"I promise," Tish said seriously.

"But even though we've come up with some ways to control your anger, you should remember that it is okay to be angry sometimes," Linda Jean assured her.

"Yeah, if no one ever got angry, problems would never be solved," Aimee added. "I mean, if we hadn't gotten mad about the person who was complaining about Linda Jean's pets, we never would have met the fun people at Orchid Gardens. And Linda Jean might still be running around after her zillion pets."

"I'm starting to see that it's not the anger in itself that's so bad," Tish said slowly. "It's what I choose to do with the anger."

"Exactly," I said with a grin.

For the next few days, Tish was great at stopping herself from getting angry. Twice at school, I saw her jotting things down in her notebook. She had a mad look on her face, so I figured she was writing down her feelings so that she could get the anger out of her system. And Aimee said that she saw Tish and her mom leaving from school together a few times in their exercise clothes.

I even caught Tish a few times at school just as she was reaching her boiling point. One day I winked at her as she was standing in line at the water fountain. She was waiting behind a guy who is the slowest drinker in the world. By winking at Tish, I think I stopped her from yelling at him or pushing his face into the water!

As I walked home from school on Friday, I thought about how great the week had gone. Tish had tried hard to keep her anger under control, and my friends had been there to help her. I was proud of them for pitching in.

I rounded the corner of my street and saw that Aimee, Linda Jean, Joy, and Tish had beaten me home. They were all sprawled on Tish's front yard. I stopped at home for a second to drop off my books and to let Mom know where I was going.

"Now I just wish that I could get up the nerve to talk to my mom and dad," Tish was saying as I sat down on the grass. "I've written down dozens of things in my notebook, but if I'm not mad when I face my parents, then I'm too nervous to talk to them."

"Well, here comes your chance," I said as I watched her parents walk out of the house.

"Oh, no!" Tish said softly. "He's carrying my notebook with all my stuff in it."

"I'd like to talk to you, Patricia," Tish's stepfather said.

"I guess we'd better go," Joy said as she started to stand up.

"No, please stay," Tish said, holding onto Joy's arm.

"But..." Joy protested as Tish's eyes pleaded with us.

"Please?" Tish begged as her stepfather walked up beside Tish.

"Yes, stay," he said. "You are all a part of this, too."

Both Mr. and Mrs. Baker sat down on the grass beside us.

"We read the things you said in your

notebook," Tish's stepdad said to her. "I think that it's really good that you're getting your feelings out on paper."

"What?" Tish asked him. "You're not mad at me?"

"Well, I would say that we're a little hurt," her mom said. "But we're not mad that you're expressing your feelings. You do accuse me and your father of some pretty terrible things, though. At least now we know what you've been keeping inside all this time."

"Have you helped Tish with this?" Tish's stepfather asked as he held up the notebook.

I didn't know what to say. I didn't want him to start yelling at us or anything. "We've been trying to help Tish understand her feelings better," I said softly.

"I think that's good," her stepdad said. "No matter what it says in this book, this is a very positive step. I'm very happy that you've been there to help Tish. And, Tish, I'm especially proud of you."

"You are?" Tish squeaked.

"So am I," Mrs. Baker agreed. "I've noticed how calm you've been around the house lately. We love you for trying so hard to adjust to your new home. We know how difficult this move has been for you."

I looked at Tish, and it was obvious that she couldn't believe what she was hearing.

"I'm really trying," she said. "I really do miss Denver and Carol a lot. But my new friends have helped me a lot, too."

Tish's stepdad said, "You know that moving isn't the easiest thing for your mother and me, either. Sometimes I feel like we just get finished unpacking and then we're moving again before we have a chance to get used to our new home."

"But you're grown-ups," Tish said. "And you're a colonel. At every new base, you have a big party. And everybody likes you and Mom. You never have any problems."

"You're wrong about that, Tish," he told her. "It hurts us to leave friends just as much as it does you. Hardly any people at work become really close friends. They try really hard to make us feel welcome, but sometimes they do that because I have a higher job than they do. They are really nice people, but that's how things often work in the military, honey."

"I never knew that," Tish admitted. "I thought I was the only one who felt scared and lonely."

"Moving isn't fun for me, either," Tish's stepdad said again. "But it's allowed me to move up in the military. To do that, I have to go where they send me."

"But we could've stayed in Denver, couldn't we?" Tish asked. Her voice cracked a little, and I thought she might cry.

"Yes, I could have retired this year, but my pension will be much better if I work for a few more years," he explained. "And then I'll be able to do all kinds of things with you and your mom. And hopefully we'll be able to stay in one place."

"Here?" Tish asked.

"I can't lie to you and promise that. But I'm going to try—that is, if we *all* like it here," Tish's stepdad grinned.

"Honey, we both love you very much," Mrs. Baker added. "It has hurt both of us to see you so sad about leaving Carol. I wanted to help, but I seemed to upset you every time I tried to say anything. I guess we all owe a big thanks to you girls for helping Tish to open up and tell us what was happening."

"Why were you reading my book?" Tish asked suddenly.

Oh, no. I was worried that Tish was going

to get mad again about her parents snooping in her things.

"I didn't mean to," Mrs. Baker explained. I was cleaning up your room, and it fell off the dresser. It landed open on the floor, and as I reached to pick it up, I saw that Mom and Dad were written everywhere. I had to know what it was. I'm sorry for reading your book, honey, but I do want you to be happy."

Tish's mom held her arms open, and Tish leaned into them for a big hug. Then she hugged her stepfather.

"Well, we were thinking about going out to dinner tonight. Would you like to go with us?" she asked Tish. "We'd love to have you girls join us, too," she asked us.

"At the officers' club?" Tish asked. I could see her stiffen up at the thought.

Her stepdad smiled and shook his head. "No. I saw a little Italian place with umbrella tables out front just a few blocks from here."

Tish hesitated. From what she had told us last weekend, her parents usually told her what to do. Asking just wasn't their way. But maybe this dinner would be a new beginning for all of them. I figured I should say something about our Forever Friends Club meeting, so the Bakers could enjoy their dinner in privacy.

"You're talking about Gino's. It's a great place," I said. "Thanks for the invitation, but Joy, Aimee, Linda Jean, and I have to finish making plans for the Tanner birthday party tomorrow. It's going to be quite a party."

"Yeah, and Tish has promised to help us," Aimee added.

"What's this all about, Tish?" her stepdad asked with a grin.

For the next 10 minutes, we filled Tish's parents in on how their daughter was going to entertain the kids with her terrific Donald Duck and Mickey Mouse impersonations. They seemed thrilled that we had included Tish in our party.

"Well, you better get to Gino's," Linda Jean said. "It gets pretty crowded."

"Try the spaghetti and clam sauce," Joy suggested. "It's my favorite."

"And don't forget the yummy garlic bread," Aimee said with a grin.

Tish giggled. "Gosh, it sounds great. I guess I can't say no, can I?"

"Yes, Tish, you can," her mom said seriously. "Sometimes, we have the right to decide what's best for you. But your opinion is always very important to this family. We'll try to do a better job of asking—and of listening. So, yes, Tish, you do have a choice."

# *Ten*

SATURDAY morning was bright and sunny. We all gathered at Abby and Joy's house extra early to make sure we had all the supplies for Lindsay Tanner's party. Tish was the third one to arrive, and she was all smiles.

"How did things go at dinner, Tish?" I asked. "From the look on your face, I would guess pretty well."

"Yeah, we talked a lot," she said. "Things aren't perfect, but I'm so happy they care enough to let me say what I think. Thanks, all of you, for helping me. I can't believe how much better I feel."

I gave her a quick hug, and then we got busy loading everything into Abby's station wagon. During the ride to the Tanners' house, we all joked and laughed about what the kids would say when Tish did her imitations.

As soon as we arrived, we had to hurry to set up everything. Lindsay's mom had requested an Old South party. The little girls were going to dress up like girls did way back in the early 1900s. We used a bicycle pump to blow up the 70 balloons, and we stood on chairs to hang colorful baskets of flowers from the tree limbs.

"Isn't it fabulous?" Tish asked excitedly, coming up behind me.

"Yeah, the decorations are great," I said.

"No, I mean the pond and the island," Tish explained. "I've never seen anything like it. Look, there are even lily pads and a floating island with a covered gazebo. It's so neat. It's like something out of a storybook."

"Yeah, Atlanta can be pretty special," I said. "Even though I've lived here all my life, I still discover neat things. I never knew that anyone could have such a huge backyard with a lake."

"Mr. Tanner said the rowboats that we can take out to the island are ready at the dock," Aimee said. "The kids should start arriving any second, so you'd better row out there now to put on the tablecloths and centerpieces."

"This is so exciting," Tish exclaimed. "I've never rowed a boat before."

I thought about how good it was to see Tish so happy and so relaxed as I climbed into the rowboat with Joy and Tish. I knew it would take a while for things to really change between Tish and her parents, but I was sure that each day would get a little better for all of them.

I looked around at my friends and giggled. I'm sure that we all looked pretty silly as we rowed toward the island. Joy was dressed in her ballerina tutu. I was wearing my clown outfit, and Tish had on her new reversible cartoon character vest.

I couldn't stop staring at Tish's vest. It was so great. Her mom had made it so that one side was black and the other side was white. She could switch it around quickly to change herself into different characters. It even had velcro tabs on it so Tish could stick on accessories like tails, spots, and a bow tie. She could quickly change into lots of different cartoon characters!

But the best thing about today was seeing a brand new Tish. She seemed so enthusiastic about everything. She couldn't seem to help us enough. If this Tish was the real Tish, then I was certain that we had a new member of The Forever Friends Club.

"Here come the kids," Joy called as we finished setting up the centerpiece. It was a lacy basket filled with fancy dried flowers and small sachet pouches that the girls could take home after the party.

Linda Jean and Aimee led Lindsay Tanner and her troop of 12 second graders across the yard to the pond. The girls were all dressed in cute, frilly dresses and matching shoes. One little girl even had her hair curled in ringlets and carried a parasol in honor of the party theme. We were doing a tea party like they had in Atlanta years ago, but we were using lemonade.

I went into the little changing tent that had been set up as Linda Jean and Aimee rowed the girls over to the island. I put on my hoop skirt for my performance. I had decided the kids would get a kick out of watching a clown try to act like a lady in an old-fashioned southern hoop skirt.

"Welcome, ladies," Aimee said to the group who was stepping out of the boat. She and Linda Jean each hopped out of the boats first so they could help the girls step onto the shore. "Please find your name cards at the tables and sit at that place."

By the time Aimee had finished having the girls decorate their name cards and their prize bags, I was ready to do my act. I stumbled out of the changing tent and walked over to the party area. I walked toward two chairs that had purposely been set up close together. They were so close that there was no way my hoop skirt could make it through the middle of them.

I made a big show of bumping into the chairs and trying to get through them. I turned sideways, and I even tried to jump over them. Finally, I held my hoop over my head and walked by the girls, so they could see my bright pink, polka dotted pantaloons that I was wearing underneath my skirt.

After I wowed them with a few magic tricks and a few crazy flips of my skirt, Joy took over and danced a butterfly dance. The girls were enchanted by her flowing, shimmering wings and the sequined cap on her head. Joy had even attached sequined antennae to her cap. She held onto a pretty parasol that had sparkly butterflies sewn onto the top.

After Joy's dance, Linda Jean brought out her furriest animals—her angora rabbits, a chinchilla, and her Teddy bear hamster. She had made another trip over to Orchid Gardens to borrow the three animals for the day. Linda Jean talked about how women in the Old South loved to dress up and go out for dinner wearing their best furs. She also pointed out how happy she was that times had changed, and that wearing furs wasn't as fashionable anymore.

Finally, it was time for Tish to do her impressions. It was difficult coming up with imitations that would match the party's theme. Kids wouldn't know the old-time actors and actresses, so we encouraged Tish to do what she knew best—Disney characters.

The party had gone perfectly—until Tish stepped up to do her act. Suddenly, everything seemed to fall apart.

Tish was wearing Mickey Mouse ears on her head, and her vest was on the black side. Stuck on her vest were the faces of several Disney characters.

"They didn't have Mickey Mouse way back in the old days," Lindsay said loudly in the middle of one of Tish's jokes.

"How do you know they didn't?" Tish asked politely.

"Because we just watched Mickey's birthday party at Disneyland, and he was only 50."

"Okay, we'll try another one," Tish said. She put on a white, George Washington wig and fancy coat with lots of braiding. "Where's my ax?" she asked in a deep voice. "I cannot tell a lie. I just chopped down the cherry tree."

Some of the kids laughed. Some of them didn't seem to have any idea what Tish was talking about. I figured the kids must not have been paying attention during their history lessons. Everyone should know about our first president.

To cover up for the kids, we all clapped as hard as we could. We hoped the kids would take the hint and clap, too. I had no idea that Tish had planned to imitate Washington. No one but the Forever Friends knew what a big deal it was for her to imitate a person. The other times we had suggested that she try to imitate a person, she had snapped at us and yelled because she didn't want to do imitations like her stepfather did. But this time she was eager to try.

"George Washington was little when he

chopped the tree." Lindsay spoke up again. "He wasn't a big man."

I wanted to put a hand over her mouth and tell her to be polite. I wondered why her parents hadn't bothered to teach her that other people have feelings, too. I looked at Tish to see how she was holding up. She looked like she was counting in her head or thinking about something to distract herself from getting mad at Lindsay.

"Can you guess who this is?" Tish asked the girls. Her voice was stern and her smile forced.

I winked at Tish, but she was too busy doing her imitation of a cartoon character from TV to pay any attention to me.

Lindsay stood up and put her hands on her hips. She turned around and grinned at her friends first, then faced Tish. "They didn't have TV either!" she said.

"Please stop being difficult, and just watch the show. Okay?" Tish snapped at her.

I was winking like crazy at Tish to get her attention. I looked over at Aimee, and she was winking and waving at Tish, too. But neither of us did any good.

"It's my party!" Lindsay yelled. "I can say

what I want!"

"Now, Lindsay," Mrs. Tanner said. She had just climbed out of the boat to see how the party was going.

"It may be your party," Tish said, "but you're not setting a very good example for your guests. I thought you were all supposed to be ladies. Ladies do not insult the entertainers for the party."

"Maybe we should have some food now," I suggested hopefully.

"You're not very funny," Lindsay cut in. "I don't want you at my party anymore."

"Well, you'll just have to put up with me," Tish shot back. "We're stuck on an island together."

"Mommy, make her go away. Make her swim away." Lindsay started pounding the table and stomping her feet on the sandy ground. She threw her noisemaker at Tish and stuck out her tongue.

"Now, Lindsay. Mind your manners," Mrs. Tanner pleaded. "Tish is doing her best to make your party fun."

"I don't have to take this. I'm leaving!" Tish said. She threw her dog ears to the ground and stomped off to the boat.

"No, you're not," I said, catching up to her and grabbing her arm. "We'll all have to talk about this later, but right now you're not going to let that little girl get the best of you. I know it's hard. She makes me mad, too. But you have to be in control of yourself, Tish. She's only a little girl."

"Little brat, you mean," Tish snapped at me.

"I've seen worse. Okay, Tish—one, two, three," I said, pretending to count to 10.

Tish finally grinned and said, "Okay, I'll stay."

\* \* \* \* \*

After we had cleaned up on the island, we rowed back across the pond to the Tanners. Abby was there waiting for us. She helped us load up the car, and we drove over to Juliet's Family Creamery for our traditional after-party celebration.

After we'd been served hot fudge sundaes, we finally felt relaxed enough to talk about the party.

"I was really proud of you for standing up to Lindsay's tantrum and going back to the party, Tish," Aimee said. "I had no idea she would be such a bossy little thing."

Joy wiped some chocolate off her face with her napkin. "I know. She practically had every kid and her mother jumping whenever she wanted something. I guess you never know how kids are going to act."

"If it was one of my little brothers, I would have sent him to his room, party or not," Aimee declared.

"I can't believe this," Tish said. "You're not mad at me? I thought I would be kicked out of The Forever Friends Club for sure this time."

"No, you did your job—and you stayed until the end," I said. "But how do you think things could have been better?" I asked her.

"I could have planned my impressions so that they matched the time period better," Tish said.

Joy shook her head. "It wouldn't have worked. The kids wouldn't have known who the people were. George Washington was about the only one that I would've thought of, too."

"Well, I could have ignored her nasty remarks and performed more to the other girls," Tish added.

"Yeah, that might have helped," Linda Jean agreed. "Sometimes when I'm showing my pets, there might be one kid who wants to be the know-it-all. I just try to ignore him or her and go on with my presentation."

"Or you can always make a joke out of it," I suggested. "If I can get the kids to laugh, they forget all the dumb comments they just made. They're really just trying to grab all the attention for themselves."

"Yeah, maybe. But I still blew it," Tish said. "You all counted on me to work with you and keep my temper under control. So what did I do? I argued with a seven year old. I don't think I'll ever get this right."

"Come on, Tish," I said, scooping out my last bite of hot fudge. "You just made one mistake. You can't expect to be perfect."

"You can't ever expect to be perfect," Joy added. "But that doesn't make you a bad person."

"I could tell stories forever about all the mistakes that I've made," Linda Jean said.

Tish was thoughtful. "You know, last night at dinner with my parents, my mom said that mistakes are just opportunities to learn something. Even she admitted that she had made a lot of mistakes before. Dad did, too."

"See. Just look at how different it was this time," Joy spoke up. "Instead of running away and ignoring the problem, you faced it. And now we're talking about different solutions together. I think that's great progress."

Tish smiled. "I guess it is. It's just so hard for me to stay and face things. It's new for me, but I'm willing to try hard at it. I'm going to need all the help I can get!"

"We'll promise to help you when you need it," I said, "If you promise to help us, too."

"It's a promise," Tish said.

We all put one hand in the center of the table. We stacked our hands like they do before sports games. The Forever Friends were like a team, too.

Tears glistened on Tish's eyelashes. "The only trouble is, I don't want to lose all of you as friends. We're probably going to move again in a couple of years. What if I never see you again?"

"I really hope that doesn't happen," I said finally. "But you'll always be a member of The Forever Friends Club. Nothing will change that."

"And you can always start a Forever Friends

Club wherever you go. It is a great way to meet people and make new friends," Linda Jean told her.

"And not only that, but we'll always stay in close contact," Aimee promised. "We'll write, call, exchange party ideas, and help each other solve problems. We'll always be there for each other."

"I think we should make a pact," Joy suggested. "I think we should decide that no matter what happens or where we go, we will always get together every five years to catch up on our lives. And we'll have reunions forever."

"I think we should make it every year," I said. "We'll take vacations from our jobs, and we'll bring along our kids."

"And our boyfriends..." added Joy.

"Or our husbands..." said Tish.

"Or our pets," Linda Jean said and giggled.

"Or even just us," Aimee said.

"Yeah. We'll have the best Forever Friends Club reunions you can imagine," I said. "Because no matter what, Forever Friends are friends forever!"

## About the Author

CINDY SAVAGE remembers what it was like to grow up with Forever Friends of her own. "We shared everything—parties, fun times, getting our ears pierced, talks about boyfriends, and really serious stuff, too. They were my best friends then, and they are still my best friends today."

Cindy's friends call themselves the Grembers of the Moop. They used to make up dances and perform for hospitals and parties—just like the Forever Friends do. One time when one of the girls was announcing the next act, she accidentally said, "And another grember of our moop..." instead of saying, "member of our group." That name stuck.

Cindy lives with her husband, Greg, and their children, Linda Jean, Laura, Warren, Brian, and Kevin, in northern California. She has a view of the beautiful Sierra Nevada Mountains from her kitchen window. When she's not writing, Cindy is a Girl Scout leader, a dancer, a cookie baker, and homework monitor. The Savage family recently welcomed Snuggles, a gray and white kitten, to their home.